THE CHRISTENING

BY THE SAME AUTHOR

The Token

THE CHRISTENING

A NOVEL

Susanna Mitchell

JOHN MURRAY

© Susanna Mitchell 1986
First published 1986
by John Murray (Publishers) Ltd
50 Albemarle Street, London W1X 4BD

All rights reserved
Unauthorised duplication
contravenes applicable laws

Typeset by Inforum Ltd, Portsmouth
Printed and bound in Great Britain
by The Bath Press, Avon

British Library CIP data
Mitchell, Susanna
The Christening: a novel.
I. Title
823'.914 [F]   PR6063.18/
ISBN 0-7195-4328-2

For Donald

I

When Miriam was away Victor always used the big bath in the room beside the nursery, finding that there he missed her less.

In their own bathroom, which was somehow so essentially *her* own bathroom, he found her absence became a vivid almost tangible thing, and the aggressive emptiness, so different from the gentle solitude of the rest of the house, made him forlorn and uneasy. He would find himself behaving quite oddly, running his hand over the stool where she sat to take off her make-up, or tracing with his finger the greasy circles left behind by all those jars and bottles, now cleared from the cluttered shelf beneath the looking glass. But nothing he did could recapture Miriam; even the light, distinctive smell that usually hung in the air – her powder, bath oil, scent? – he did not know what caused it, never lingered behind her to keep him company. With Miriam gone the room was alien to him: without her reflection to fill it, the mirrored wall became merely tawdry, the sliding door bare and ugly without her dressing gown; and all those matching fittings in gleaming maroon, which he hardly noticed when her beauty and colour and vitality were there to distract him, struck him as both dismal and vulgar when he had to face them alone. Once or twice he had found it hard to dispel the faint, disloyal thought that perhaps he should not have allowed Miriam such a free hand with her various improvements, most of which had ended up so strangely out of keeping with the atmosphere at Coombe. But such feelings were purely superficial; in his heart he could never regret her delight in her achievements, he only wished that the early interest and excitement had not died away. Perhaps that was why her bathroom made him so uneasy? It seemed to embody a Miriam mysteriously lost.

In any case, he found it better to start these dismal wifeless mornings in what they always called the West Room, where Great-grandfather's magnificent folly of a bath stood massively in the middle of the floor. Originally it had been meant for another, less commodious bedroom, somewhere at the back of the house, but it had proved too large to be hoisted in, except through the wide bay window of the West Room, and there it had remained. Its curved enamel shower, cast in one piece with the rest, soared up towards the tangle of plumbing that hung from the ceiling, and a metal nozzle, green with age and tarnish, protruded incongruously from the elegant plasterwork of the moulding above. There was no longer a bed, but no one had ever troubled to take away the rest of the furniture, and Victor loved the solid dignified way the bath had settled in among the heavy mahogany and faded Persian runners, making itself completely at home. It was true that the drainage sometimes behaved in an alarming manner, and that the pipes, whistling and juddering with effort, would surrender only a tepid stream of water, but in view of its distance from the drains and the boiler, it was a considerable triumph that the whole thing worked at all.

This morning, as he lay in the shallows with the familiar chill of unheated enamel creeping along his spine, Victor tried to surrender himself to the soothing quality of the West Room, which could always be relied upon to reaffirm the purpose and pattern of his life.

It was not that he questioned his affection for Coombe. He loved his house with its sunny passages and graceful staircase, and the smell of polished floor boards and wood smoke that hung faintly about the high, well-proportioned rooms. He was proud of his park and gardens and the rolling farm land, of his river and his beech woods, and above all of the stables where his dearest interests lay. He felt a pleasant responsibility towards his tenant farmers, and was gratified to find that Coombe Abbott and Coombe Bassett looked so prosperous, since the greater part of both villages was still owned by him. But these days, without quite understanding what was missing, he had lost the unquestioning complacency that had always sustained his family. Sometimes, despite the astounding delights of his marriage, he did notice the lack of his old comfortable self-assurance, and wondered uneasily why it should have gone?

In Great-grandfather's bath, however, he could be certain of finding a trace of it to encourage him. Its placid air of confidence made a nonsense of regrets and lost opportunities, ignored the existence of turmoil or diffidence or doubt. In the West Room it seemed unfitting to wonder, as lately he found himself doing elsewhere, whether his career would have fulfilled its promise if Jamie had not died? Here, such a thought became a weakness amounting almost to betrayal, for what career could have been more suitable, more rewarding, than preserving Coombe for future generations of Templetons?

He smiled, thinking of the baby, and began to wrestle with the obstinate metal plunger that blocked the outlet pipe. When he was dressed, he would go straight to the nursery, and perhaps that ferocious Nanny Miriam had engaged would allow him to hold the baby while he fed. He missed watching the baby feeding: he would never forget how wonderful it had been, in the beginning, when Miriam had fed him herself. It had been thrilling to see her, propped up in their big bed where he himself had been suckled, looking so radiant and tender, with their son at her breast. It was a shame that she had wanted to wean him so soon.

For a moment he stood motionless, staring down at the corkscrew spiral of water that now revolved obediently round the drain. There were times when he perceived, with a clarity almost akin to terror, how urgently Miriam needed to feel herself free. Had he been unforgivably selfish in marrying her, a man in his middle forties, whose life was fixed in a mould that no girl could find anything but dull? She was so young and beautiful and talented, he could not expect her to confine herself to this house where she could see no challenge or scope; it was no wonder that, in certain moods, she found the significance it held for him hard to comprehend. What had she said about this bathroom, for instance? 'How typically arrogant!' Yes. That was what she'd said.

He climbed out slowly. Well, perhaps it was arrogant. Perhaps that was what he found so comforting: and how pleasing it would be to see his son – several sons, in fact, and a few daughters thrown in for good measure, piled into the capacious tub. He could imagine them there quite plainly, laughing and splashing and turning somersaults on the long parallel handles of the shower shield, as he and Jamie and the girls had so often done.

He picked up the towel briskly. There was a lot to be done this morning. He hoped Miriam would not be too late coming home. It was not her fault, of course, but her audition had certainly arisen at a most inconvenient moment, with the christening already fixed for tomorrow, and so many people coming to stay. Still, never mind: he was sure that they could manage, and he was looking forward very much to seeing his child baptised.

James Alexander Richard Templeton. James for Jamie. Alexander after Father. And Richard, rather less happily, as a gesture to Miriam's father, poor old Dickie Bernstein, who had so disastrously married Cousin Grace; though he must try to cure himself of the family habit of calling the match disastrous, since without it Miriam would not be there to delight him. How extraordinary life could be! And how plucky Miriam had been about it all, the appalling embezzlement scandal, the embarrassment of the divorce. He supposed the level-headedness of the Templetons had come through in the blood and had strengthened her, though heaven knew it was hardly much in evidence in the character of Cousin Grace. Anyway, he could hardly be stuffy about Dickie if Miriam stood by him so gamely, and besides he admired her for it, he would never want anyone to reject their kith and kin. He only hoped that their baby would grow up as loyal and forgiving as his mother. James Alexander. His son. It made the whole decision, sometimes bewilderingly unsatisfactory during his years of bachelorhood, entirely worth while.

It had been a momentous decision: he saw that now, though at the time of Jamie's death, and with Father so ill, he had hardly looked on his homecoming in that light. Viewed through his shock and grief, his promising future in the Navy had become as unreal as his childhood's dream of being a polar explorer, and the painstaking effort he had made to disinterest himself in Coombe in order to avoid interfering in Jamie's management had collapsed on the instant as if it had never been. Stunned by the loss of his brother, moved by his father's helplessness and despair, he had simply followed his instinctive reaction. Within three months of the accident, on the eve of his thirtieth birthday, he had resigned his commission and come back to live at home.

He rubbed himself vigorously, banishing the memory of those painful years of readjustment. It had all been worth while: tomorrow his baby would be christened. And if he felt pleasure at the discomforture of his sister Hester, he was determined not to feel guilty about it. After all the unkind things she had said about Miriam, he would have to be a saint not to derive some gratification that it was going to be their son, and not hers, who would one day inherit Coombe.

It was a pity that neither of his sisters had really got to know Miriam, though of course, being so much older, there was not much common ground. Lizzie was wrapped up in her children, and Hester was naturally diffident; besides, her whole existence was based on the hope that her son, her rather dull son Edward, would eventually live at Coombe Manor. Dear old Dorothy, on the other hand, had bridged the gap pretty well; but then Dorothy had nothing to lose, she was simply a childhood acquaintance, and she had always been sensitive to other people's feelings; too sensitive perhaps. That distressing breakdown; he wondered sometimes if she had fully recovered. In any case, he was most relieved that Miriam had agreed to ask her to be a Godmother; that seemed to have pleased her enormously. It was good to see her happy, for really she had been as much a part of his childhood as Jamie and Hester and Lizzie. Why, when they were all very tiny she had even used this bath! Poor Dorothy. Even then she had been a self-conscious little thing, and her sight had always been bad. He could still picture those ugly, owlish spectacles with the wire ear pieces, from which she would not be parted. She used to hide before the communal bathtimes, knowing that her glasses would be taken from her, afraid that she would be laughed at for bumping into things; and when she had been found she had always been punished, for flouting authority was not encouraged in the Templeton nursery. Yet he, who alone had understood, had not explained her fear to Nanny; it had seemed to him then that Dorothy would prefer to be laughed at because she was naughty than because she was frightened, and Nanny had never been discreet.

Now, with the new protective insight that being a father had given him, he suddenly wondered anxiously whether he had been right. It was a pity you couldn't ask Dorothy that sort of question: it was still all too easy to throw her into confusion, and recollections of her playing naked with his sisters would certainly be a mistake. Instead he would underline their intimacy by having a word with her about Hester and William. He knew she would understand, and do her best to make the day go smoothly for all of them, even to the extent of seeing that, as far as possible, Hester and Miriam were kept apart.

He crossed to the window, casting aside the thought of his family's intransigence, and flung up the sash. Wispy vapour still clung round the trees in the park, but behind him he knew that the sun was just rising, for the flat pearl grey of the mist was fluid with gold. Such glorious weather for October! It had gone on for weeks now, day after cloudless day.

He leant out as far as he could, with his hands on the cold stone of the windowsill, and gazed up into the brightening sky. Surely it was his imagination that today the dawn felt less crisp and buoyant, altogether heavier? It would be so disappointing if the fine spell broke just before the christening. He wanted Coombe to be at its best for James Alexander; the autumn light breathtaking on the stubble fields and the turning beeches; the little chapel filled with welcome and sun. In fact he was amazed at the significance that tomorrow held for him. He felt quite alarmed at the thought of anything going wrong, of anything spoiling the perfection of what he had come to look upon as a uniquely important day.

He drew back, shivering, irritated by his own anxiety, shamed by the strength of his childish superstition. He must get on: he would spoil the day himself if he idled up here any longer when so many jobs were waiting to be done. It was a mercy, really, that the last disagreement had blown over and Mrs Scott had agreed to stay. She would manage her part in the preparations beautifully, encouraged by the prospect of putting up Hester and Lizzie, and hearing their unstinted praise of all the work she had done. She was quite devoted to both his sisters; in fact since Mother's death he knew that she regarded the family almost as if they were her own. She had been at Coombe a long time now, almost forty years, he supposed. He could hardly remember the place without her, and yet for some reason he did not share the warm affection displayed by Hester and Lizzie, and it irked him to hear them continually congratulate and admire her, as if her business in his house was a charitable enterprise, and he himself a dependent child. It was particularly clear at such moments that for Mrs Scott nothing could make up for the fact that he was not Jamie, once and for ever the apple of her eye. Jamie's good taste, his sociability, his accuracy as a shot, his prowess as a public speaker, even the unfailing instinct that enabled him to fill Coombe with an undiluted selection of the Right People – he had observed all these traits in his brother, but had never felt overshadowed by them while he was alive. It was doubly annoying therefore, to find that the Jamie of Mrs Scott's fond recollection, who fluttered ghostlily between them every time he came to a decision of any importance, always watched him with pity and reproof.

It had hardly come as a surprise, when he first married Miriam, to find that Mrs Scott had taken a profound dislike to her, and at the time he had not really been sorry. It made it easier, indeed essential to dismiss her at once. He need feel no qualm about the rights or wrongs of it either, for no one could be expected to employ a housekeeper who showed unveiled hostility towards his wife. It would have been worse in the long run, he had reflected cheerfully, if Mrs Scott had tried to be respectful and pleasant, for now that he was married she was not needed any more. Her ability to run his home would simply be wasted, for Miriam, as mistress of Coombe, would naturally want to take over all her most hallowed duties, like ordering the meals and interviewing the staff; in the end, Mrs Scott would inevitably have felt usurped. How much better it would be, he had said to Miriam, for her to engage some younger, more malleable woman, and train her to run Coombe exactly as she wanted it run.

He still could not understand why Miriam had instantly quashed all thought of Mrs Scott's departure, had begged him almost angrily to leave things as they were. Perhaps she was unwilling or afraid to tackle the responsibilities of her position? Perhaps she did not see how important it was to him that she should be interested and involved? Now that he came to think of it, it was rather as if she looked on Coombe as a well-run country hotel where she happened to be spending a prolonged visit, and where Mrs Scott, as manageress, was satisfactory enough.

He sighed. If only Miriam were here he would not be a prey to these hurtful, disquieting feelings. What did it matter if tomorrow the flowers were arranged by Dorothy, the food planned and selected by Mrs Scott? What did it matter that when his sisters arrived Miriam would not even know in which room their families were sleeping, that the little gifts for Lizzie's children had been bought and parcelled by himself? It did not matter: it mattered not one jot so long as Miriam was there beside him, desirable and passionate, entrancingly young and ardent, and by some unbelievable good fortune actually his wife and the mother of his son. It was, after all, rather wonderful, the curious atmosphere of unreality with which she invested his house and gardens, as if she had turned them into a stage setting, a fairytale backdrop for their love affair.

As he opened the door, he became aware that the telephone was ringing, and a surge of happy anticipation scattered his reverie. He knew it would be Miriam; how dear, how caring of her to phone him! It was just what he needed when, for no known reason, he was feeling so confused and depressed. He was instantly terrified that she would ring off before he could reach the receiver. Their bedroom? Or the telephone that stood on the hall table? It was less private, but probably nearer. He raced down the stairs towards it, taking them two at a time.

"Hello?" he said breathlessly, snatching the earpiece from its cradle. "Hello? Are you there? Is that you, Miriam?" How awful if he had abused this loving gesture, had caught the telephone on its last despairing ring.

He could picture her so vividly, her fair hair uncombed and tousled as he loved to see it, her face naked of make up, smooth and innocent as a child's. He longed to reach out and touch her, but her voice at least would foster the illusion that she was with him. He could hardly wait to hear it, for it to break the loneliness of the empty hall.

"It's Dorothy," said the telephone. "Have I woken you? I know it's very early, Victor. . ."

He could have slammed down the receiver, he felt such disappointment. Yet it was nice of Dorothy to ring him, when she had so much to do before she left for school.

"Oh . . . Dorothy!" he said with an effort. "No, I wasn't asleep. As a matter of fact I've been up for ages. I was taking a dip in the Biggest Bath in the World."

Why had he said that? Her whimsey must be infectious. It was absurd to regress to the phrases of their childhood, a nauseating attempt at baby talk: and now, as he feared, he had made her coy and confidential.

"Why, Victor," she was saying, "how lovely. Did you turn somersaults between the handles? I was sure Miriam said you didn't use that bath any more."

"Well, I do sometimes," he said, making his voice as distant and reserved as possible, "just to see that the plumbing's still working." A worrying thought assailed him, and he added irritably, "What's the matter anyway, Dorothy? You are coming to do the flowers?" Dreadful to be dependent on Dorothy to make the house look bright and cared for, maybe he could learn to do the flowers himself?

"Yes, of course I am." She sounded pleased, motherly and reassuring. "I was just ringing to tell you I'd be round after school to do them, and not to worry if I'm a bit late. And I wondered if it would help if I collected the wine in Hungerford? It might give you one less thing to do when you are all alone."

The 'all alone' was emphatic, heavy with criticism of Miriam's absence.

"I've got to go there anyway," he said untruthfully, "so don't worry, Dorothy, I'll pick it up myself. There's nothing to do here that bothers me anyway. Miriam's left everything very cut and dried. . ."

"Oh!" said Dorothy, and he was pleased to hear that she was disappointed. "Well, that's all right then, Victor. I just wondered if I could help. And I didn't want you to fret," she was rallying now, confident of her usefulness, "if I seem a little late this evening. Nurse Rose says she'll stay on till seven, and so I'll have plenty of time."

He went back upstairs slowly, feeling ten years older than when he had rushed down them. Thank goodness Miriam would be back in time to help him cope with Dorothy; she made him feel quite uneasy these days, though he couldn't exactly say why. He hoped her flower arrangements would turn out as she wanted, for otherwise she would weep, he was sure, and have to be soothed and comforted; and Miriam, who had not known her before her breakdown, would declare how trying she was.

He opened the nursery door softly and left it ajar behind him, hoping Nanny would not notice the draught. That way, he would be sure to hear the bell ringing if Miriam, after all, decided to telephone him.

2

"It sounds as if you might get it," said Justin from the pavement.

Below him in the basement, Miriam slammed the front door and turned round to double lock it, determined to pay no attention to the insincerity of his tone. She would take the words at their face value and betray nothing of her irritation. With her back safely towards him she relieved her feelings by pulling a horrible face. She felt hot and exhausted; it had taken her a long time to load the car, and some of the luggage had been exceptionally awkward and heavy. She knew Justin had noticed that she could barely lift the boxes of groceries, and had not been blind to her struggles with the christening cake and the new cot either: but he had not offered to help her, and she had not humbled herself by asking, as no doubt he hoped she would do.

Instead she had spoken in a desultory way about her audition, throwing her remarks up and down the area steps, hoping that by this haphazard treatment she might make the whole affair sound both less important to her, and at the same time more promising, than it really was; but he had seen through that at once, she could tell by the sweetly compliant way he carried on his half of the conversation. She knew he would have grilled her for details if he thought she stood a chance.

She turned and glanced up at him where he waited, leaning against the railings.

"Oh, I don't know," she said vaguely, as if her mind was drifting to more important matters. "I expect I might, but you never can tell, can you? Anyway it was fun doing it. Though I wish they could have chosen a more convenient day."

"Well, speak for yourself," he said. "A free lift door to door suits me nicely."

He paused and then added with studied lightness, "Perhaps it might be better if I kept my own keys?"

She flushed and took them from her bag, tossing them up to him with an angry flick of her wrist. What a silly mistake to make, and how petty it all was, this business of the keys! When she married Victor it had seemed almost symbolic to give her own set to Justin, since there had been nothing else she could do that would adequately mark the break. In fact, she had soon seen it was simply pointless and inconvenient to be without them, though to ask for them back was entirely impossible: that would be to admit that the gesture had been foolish and melodramatic, which was exactly how Justin had described it at the time.

She watched him catch the keys easily and gracefully, barely shifting his position, not bothering to uncross his legs. Suddenly she wished very much that she had not persuaded Victor to let him stand as Godfather to the baby, indeed that she had not asked him to come to Coombe for the christening at all. She had hardly looked at him while she was packing the Volvo, hoping that her disregard would undermine his efforts to annoy her, but now she realised that he had changed into a particularly dreadful T-shirt, black with some sick transfer of skulls printed all over the front in luminous shades of green and orange and fuchsia. Somehow his jeans looked tighter than ever, his sneakers older, his hair more obviously bleached and artificial. He had made himself as ludicrous, as unacceptable as possible: he was baiting her yet again to reject him, to concede that she was ashamed to produce him like that at Coombe. The T-shirt alone was as good as a speaking challenge: she must stand by him at his worst or discard him absolutely. To win the game she must pretend neither to notice, nor care, that his clothes were unsuitable; she must not ask whether he had brought something different to wear tomorrow at the church. If she did, then he would see it as a sort of victory, an admission that he might disgrace her in her new life. He would say he had known from the beginning that she would come to feel like this about him, and had always told her so.

She began to climb the steep steps towards him, jerking her suitcase clumsily up the bottom stairs towards the curve of the iron bannister. Her head throbbed with anger and disappointment. Why couldn't Justin make some effort to trust her, when she had tried so hard to prove her loyalty to him? He had been really pleased when she had asked him to be the baby's Godfather; she was sure of that, though he had quickly turned the whole thing into a joke. But now, it seemed, he was determined to repudiate his own pleasure and embarrass her by showing everybody that he regarded the christening as nothing more than a ridiculous farce. Well, she thought so too, in a way; that was why it should have been so heartening to have him there beside her. Why couldn't he help her to carry it through instead of being antagonistic? He must know that she had only asked him to come as a mark of faith in their continuing friendship; it was absurd of him to pretend she was taking baptism seriously herself.

The bend was sharp, and the case, dragging behind her at an angle, had jammed itself between the metal uprights of the handrail. She stepped over it and tugged at it furiously, staggering drunkenly backwards as its weight became free.

"Oh, Christ!" said Justin.

He sounded exasperated beyond endurance, but he must have moved astonishingly quickly, for he reached her before the end of the long second during which her balance still hung in doubt. He gripped her arm roughly in one hand and her suitcase in the other, and hauled them both on to the pavement at his side.

"You'd kill yourself first, wouldn't you?" he burst out angrily. "You'd break your skull open down there, before you'd ask for a hand from me! You're just pigheaded, Miriam; immature, spiteful, stupid!"

He had not relaxed his hold and now he shook her as he finished speaking, as if to emphasise his words.

Pigheaded. Immature. For a moment the sheer audacity of it choked her. And spiteful too, of all things to say! Who had been spiteful enough to loaf around while she sweated and struggled up and down the steps, taunting her with insolent unhelpfulness, trying to goad her into protest or tears? Who had been immature enough to start this silly childish charade? Justin himself. Justin as usual. He was outrageous. She really couldn't stand him one second longer.

It was not until she squirmed round in his grip, swinging up her free hand to push him away from her, wishing she was strong enough to spreadeagle him on the pavement, that she looked into his face: and at once, as so often happened in her dealings with Justin, she knew that she had lost. How could she remain angry when she saw what a fright she had given him, when she knew that his rudeness was just an expression of his guilt and alarm, and of his abrupt disenchantment with the game they had both been playing? For of course she had been playing it too; why else had she not asked him to help her, naturally and simply, as she would have asked Victor?

She dropped her hand hopelessly. What was the point in apportioning the blame? She knew quite well that they were both pigheaded and spiteful, and now that her resentment was spent she also realised that she felt rather giddy; it had been a nasty moment there on the area steps. The air was becoming so close and muggy, perhaps that was why they were both irritable. She sagged against Justin wearily, resting her cheek on his chest. The aggressive T-shirt was no longer offensive to her. She was aware only of the familiar curve of the hard dancer's muscles, warm and solid against her face.

It was always the same: once they were over she could never remember why they had become involved in these bitter, yet curiously artificial quarrels, which in retrospect seemed like scenes from some unintelligible play. What had she been trying to prove? It was always useless to hide her real emotions from him anyway, or pretend to misread his response: no one understood her, no one saw through her, like Justin. Victor now, dear, adoring, gullible Victor – if he had watched her during this last half hour he would have fallen for her act completely, have assumed she had achieved both the audition and the packing without anxiety or effort. He would never have been sceptical of the show she was putting on. Though of course, with Victor around, such a situation could never have arisen. When had he let her lift a feather without rushing to her aid?

The thought disturbed her and she drew away from Justin, glancing uneasily at the pretty enamel watch that Victor had given her when the baby was born. He would be waiting, impatient, loving, longing for her return. She must not allow herself to find his trust or his protective attention cloying, must not feel smothered by the devotion she had sought so long to find. Life with Justin had been a mess, a distressing complicated mess without any prospect of a future, and she must not for a moment forget how unsatisfactory it had become. It was dishonest and sentimental to remember only the good things, and particularly false to dwell on the affinity that had always united them and now seemed so obstinately resistant to change. After all, it had not been enough. It had not made up for the poverty and insecurity of their hand-to-mouth existence, all the things that she wanted to buy, all the places she wanted to see. She had hoped things might improve when Justin was made a principal, but it hadn't made much difference, with the debts piled up behind them and her own parts so hard to find. And that had not been easy either, being out of work when he was in constant training. He had had no time to spare for sociability or entertainment, and no energy over to make a fuss of her, or sympathise about the scarcity of plays. He hardly seemed to notice the soul-destroying jobs she took on to keep them in some kind of comfort: he was always brittle with exhaustion or on one of those highs she no longer found so alluring, and either way he was maddeningly oblivious to the squalid depths of their living standards, to their lack of possessions, to how little chance they stood of getting anywhere in life. What hope of security, let alone of leisure or luxury, could she possibly have had if she had stayed with

Justin? She was tired of buses and basements, of bills and old clothes and of being nobody; she had been more than justified in putting an end to so many wasted years.

Surely, after such a long affair, she could expect to keep up a civilised and rewarding friendship? She must try to be more detached about it, and make sure that it did not disturb the tenor of her life with Victor. What did it matter if sometimes she had to humour Justin along?

"Why don't you drive?" she said.

She knew he liked driving the Volvo despite the way he sneered at it, but she seldom suggested that he took the wheel; why should she, when he was so scathing about everything it represented? She still felt piqued at the memory of his initial amusement, at how foolish he had made her feel the first time she had met him at the station, when he had come prancing out of the train wearing his ridiculous alpaca coat.

"Dog-guards!" he had cried. "Labradors! Oiled shooting jackets! Well, you've certainly set it up thoroughly – every cliché in the book! But you can't have forgotten . . ." pausing and peering disgustedly in at the back window, "you can't have forgotten the pair of pale green wellies? Why no, there they are! Oh, it's perfect, Miriam darling. Keep up the good work and you'll find you blend into it nicely. There'll be nothing left of you soon except a huskie and a headscarf, propped up behind the wheel."

Everyone within earshot had turned to look at him, and she had not blamed them. That coat always cried out for attention and she knew that was exactly why he had chosen it to bring down to Coombe. It swept almost to the ground, shabby and yet garish, covered with delapidated embroidery, trimmed with what looked like dirty cotton wool. How did he manage to make it look so natural, so dashing? For some reason it only added to her resentment to know that no one else at the station could have carried off such a preposterous garment. With its wide skirts flapping around him, even Victor would have been reduced to a figure of fun.

Now, looking back, she wondered if it was the coat, and the

way he had used it to score a point off Victor, that had upset her, for surely she had not really minded his remarks about the car? She had wanted nothing more, in those days, than to blend into the background of the Volvo, to lose herself in the cloud of prosperous self-assurance that it guaranteed. She had been thankful to feel that in it she was classified and protected, indistinguishable from all those other wives in estate cars who were constantly visiting Coombe.

She sighed: it was no time ago, yet her viewpoint did seem to have altered. She glanced through the window, catching sight of herself in the curve of the wing mirror. She was pleased with her new hairstyle, it made her feel much younger and trendier, almost as if she had never had the baby. She hoped that Victor would like it too. Justin had been surprisingly enthusiastic, but then that was hardly the same thing; in fact it probably meant that she had ruined her efforts to look suitable and settled in front of all Victor's relations tomorrow, that she had made another mistake. It was annoying to find that 'blending in' was more difficult than she had expected; she had never thought it would be so hard to achieve, or that, once accomplished, the experience would prove quite so dull. She had not anticipated the feeling of boredom and restlessness which seemed to grow in exact proportion to her success as a country wife, or the curious impulse to shock which seized her when anyone showed signs of thawing into friendship. Suddenly it occurred to her that she might be more like her mother than she had ever realised. What had Mother's marriage been, if not an act of rebellion? But then, from the start, it had gone sadly wrong, and in view of that and the state that Mother was in nowadays, the discovery of a latent resemblance was hardly a pleasant idea.

She abandoned it hastily, but the train of thought led her to another unsatisfactory subject.

"Dad's coming down tomorrow," she remarked, and instantly wished the words unsaid. She had not meant to mention her father when Justin was in this mood, but of course he had heard her and pounced on it at once.

"Dickie's coming?" he said. "Honestly, Miriam! You really are a glutton for punishment, aren't you? Surely you could have managed to put him off?" He sounded outraged by her stupidity.

"Shall I tell you what he'll do?" he went on angrily, and ignored her silence as if it had been an assent. "Well, first he'll get stoned, absolutely sozzled. You know he can't stop now, even if he wanted to? And then he'll start on his grievances as usual ... how he should never have been convicted, how people shun and misunderstand him. And of course, how really it's because he's Jewish – and not because he's a boring, lecherous old fraud."

He paused, and she thought he had finished: but it seemed she was not to get off so lightly. He was just getting into his stride.

"At this point," he continued, "he'll start to shout. He'll say we all should know what it's like to be in prison, and then he'll tell us. Loudly. Fully. Interminably, it will seem. But at last he'll start to weep, and look round for female comfort. Who do you think he'll choose to feel up this time, Miriam? How about that sister of Victor's – the one who looks as if the drains aren't working properly? Or that batty old bird you've asked to be a Godmother?" He laughed mirthlessly. "What a prospect! I can hardly wait to see their faces."

Miriam sat stiffly, her face turned away from him, and groped in vain for something to say. Anything would do, so long as it stopped him. But the shattering rehearsal of Dad's behaviour tomorrow seemed to have paralysed her, and her mind was empty and blank. Instead she stared out of the window. Beneath the flyover, the little houses stretched away in monotonous rows, more hideous and hopeless than ever under the yellowing sky. No use in pretending the fine weather was not breaking.

"There's going to be a storm," she said at last.

Perhaps that would change the subject? Perhaps it would even right the balance a little, for she knew Justin was terrified of thunder. But her throat was oddly constricted, and her voice came out as a whisper. He gave no sign that he had heard her speak.

"I thought I was to be the bad fairy," he was saying sarcastically. "But I tell you, I'll be nothing beside dear old Dickie! I can't understand it. Why the hell did you say that you'd have him? You must have gone completely nuts."

She glanced at him sideways, taking in the line of his jaw, set rigidly to convey his complete incomprehension. At least that was a transparent piece of pretence; however sincere his determination not to help her, she could never believe he had forgotten so much of their mutual past.

"You know quite well why he's coming," she said bitterly. "You know what it does to me when he really pulls the stops out. And I tell you I got the whole performance when he heard about the christening. I've seldom seen him put on a better show."

She paused, assailed by the memory of Dickie in his role of rejected parent. The sick old man. He'd had a cold too, which made the part easier and more convincing. The sick old man, bowed with sorrows, victim of undeserved misfortune, abandoned by his friends and spurned by his family, his good works and devotion all forgotten: cut to the quick, yet too noble and unselfish to bear anybody malice – but oh, the cruelty, the injustice of the world! It had certainly been exaggerated, she could not believe that some shadow of the old Dickie did not delight in playing this travesty of a father, but there was enough truth there to move her nonetheless. He *had* had a lot to bear, however badly he had taken it, and he was genuinely hurt and offended at the thought she might push him aside. She couldn't cold-shoulder him like that, though part of her knew that he thoroughly deserved it. Besides, she had assumed that Justin would support her, he had always had such a genius for handling Dickie: now it seemed that for once he was going to let her down. She felt angry and bereft, caught between the spectre of sad unacceptable Father and the reality of Justin, hostile in the clothes he had chosen to underline her shame.

There was a long silence. Justin changed gear deftly and

eased the car forward onto the motorway. After a moment he dropped his hand from the steering wheel and laid it upon her knee.

"Well, I've put my suit in the back," he said. "And a clean shirt. And those shoes that give me blisters. And I've bought a present for your baby. The Complete Dictionary of Music. Two volumes in leather bindings. It cost us quite a bit."

Her heart lifted at once; how could she have been so mistaken? The words were a promise, however obliquely phrased. They affirmed that he stood behind her, and at once all her confidence in him was reasserted, despite that involuntary 'us' of which he seemed unconscious; or perhaps because of it, and his hand upon her knee?

He would not let her down, though of course it wasn't particularly important – not these days, when she'd Victor there standing in the wings. She lowered the window and let the air stream round her, cooling her flushed face. The sky was certainly oppressive, such an evil and disagreeable colour, but the storm would probably blow itself out quite soon. It would leave the air crisp and refreshed, and the sun would break through and enliven the gathering tomorrow. Dad might even emerge as the life and soul of the party in the way that he once would have done. And she would enjoy herself too: it would be fun flaunting Jamie before all those stuffy relations.

Her hand fell absently, resting on top of Justin's: it was pleasing to know he'd reacted according to plan. In fact it was difficult to explain why she had felt so agitated. She was bringing a friend to a family celebration; and she'd got the lead, she could handle the thing very nicely. There was nothing at all that was likely to go wrong.

3

Dorothy hated storms. She had known all afternoon that one was gathering: had known it, to be precise, since the moment she had glanced upwards as she crossed the quadrangle at lunch time, eager to escape from the scuffed walls and the drab tarmac, and the heavy smell coming from the school canteen.

The fine weather had lasted long enough to lull her into confidence. She had been sure that she would find a fragment of the exquisite Indian summer framed, as usual, in the concrete square above her head. Instead, where the faraway bowl of the sky should have arched harmlessly above her, she had seen the first white haze gathering, stealthily forming over the blue. That had been the beginning, the first of the many colour washes that would darken and drag down the sky. For hours she had known that it was thickening and falling lower, until now as she craned out of her form room window, it seemed to sag all around her, yellow and sticky with thunder, like the canvas of some huge collapsing tent.

She withdrew her head and pressed her hands to her temples. The humidity had made her eyes heavy, had sapped her determination, and it was always such an effort to reach the car park once the final bell had sounded. The stairs and corridors would be surging with bodies, shoving and shouting their way out of the buildings, milling into the bedlam of the playground below.

How could these children be so different? At Frampton Hall, the girls had certainly been lively and sometimes noisy: one or two had occasionally been boisterous or impolite – but that was all. Never had she imagined, never had she thought to see, hundreds of children falling into an uncontrolled state of frenzy. Yet here, day after day, she watched it happen; watched them yelling and pushing and knocking each other over, throwing insults and books, stones and schoolbags.

Each afternoon, as she edged her way through them, she felt herself more and more repelled by their behaviour, more and more estranged. She was ashamed too, distressed by the injustice of her own reaction. It was appalling that she could feel such animosity towards children. She had always thought she loved them unconditionally, reserving a special place in her heart for those who were difficult or misunderstood. Here, in this shabby overcrowded comprehensive school, she should have found a new and stimulating challenge, and instead she was harbouring cruel and unworthy feelings. It was quite dreadful to regard these youngsters as not only different but inferior, when she knew that in the eyes of the Lord . . . but since she had become afraid, since the day when her glasses, knocked off in a collision, had been trampled upon before they could be salvaged so that she stood in the chaos virtually blind and helpless, she knew that the wickedness would constantly be with her, alienating her from her true self.

She supposed it was simply an extension of that wickedness that had prompted her to be interviewed for the post at Gaston Abbey, knowing all the time that she could never accept a job that would mean closing the house and sending Father away to live with Aunt Maud. She had worried a lot about it lately, trying to analyse her sinful perseverance in what was only a fantasy of escape.

She forgave herself the first letter, even the first interview. All that had simply been an exercise in make believe, an antidote to desperation from which she had expected no actual result. It had been wonderful to have something interesting to do for a few days during the holidays, and Nurse Rose had already offered to let her away for a short break. She had driven up to Shropshire with a sense of dreamlike unreality, and found Gaston Abbey as enchanting as she had instinctively known it would be. In the familiar congenial atmosphere she had faced her interview blithely. After all there was nothing to be nervous about, since she could not possibly take the job, and there were so many applicants that she felt one more could hardly matter to anybody: but at this point all excusable behaviour ended. She could not imagine what evil impulse had carried her back to Shropshire when she had found she was short-listed, and sustained her cheerfully through a second and now unpardonably deceitful interview. They had been so kind too, the Headmistress and the Board of Governors, and most appreciative of her successful years at Frampton Hall. What on earth would she say to them if now, by any chance, they decided to offer her the position? These last few days she had grown to dread the arrival of her mail. But she must not think of that now, not when such a delightful weekend was coming.

She combed her hair furtively with her back turned to the doorway, and dabbed her powder puff blindly over her nose. She would have liked to wash her hands and to splash her forehead with cold water, but that would have meant going all the way to the staff cloakroom at the other end of the corridor. She couldn't face that: it was bad enough to think of struggling to the car park through the very centre of the explosion down below her; and today she must not linger, not when Victor was depending on her coming as soon as she could. She filled a plastic carrier with books and squared her shoulders resolutely. If she fixed her mind on the happy hours before her, she hoped that the playground would not seem so bad.

The car park lay beyond the school buildings on a narrow strip of waste ground, bounded on one side by the perimeter wall and on the other by the high windowless back of the gymnasium. She had been disgusted, on the first day of her appointment, to find that these walls were used by the school as a sort of unofficial notice board. The graffiti were unpleasantly crude and insolent; disgraceful comments upon the staff, smutty allusions to crushes between pupils, and drawings from which she hastily turned her eyes. Of course there were regular scrubbing parties, but the new overspill community had crammed the school with a flood of disoriented children, who seemed determined to express themselves in this way.

Today, as she rounded the corner, she was painfully aware

that the walls were again defiled, but at least she had reached the car without incident and now only a short journey lay between her and the safety of Coombe. She placed her bag of books thankfully on the bonnet and flexed her stiff fingers: all that remained was to get out the keys of the car.

She opened her bag and groped about in it blindly, a familiar little spurt of panic rising in her chest. The house key, the garage key, the key of the staff locker: her damp fingers defined them and pushed them back again. How dreadful if she had left them behind her in the classroom! It would make her impossibly late to go all the way back through the playground, and then she would never have time to do the flower arrangements properly. There was barely a moment to waste as it was, with the traffic so dreadful and Nurse Rose to relieve at seven. Oh, what should she do? And why could she not see better? Perhaps it would be worth while changing quickly to her reading glasses? But she couldn't feel them either, maybe she had put them in the plastic bag. How she wished she were back at Frampton Hall, where she could ask some friendly girl to come and help her. The very thought of those lost solicitous faces made the tears prick behind her eyes.

Down the row of cars she could hear other members of staff calling out to each other, laughing and chatting, banging doors and revving engines. How could they bear to linger and joke in the car park, when these horrible things were around them on the walls?

"Lost something, Dorothy?"

She jerked round, startled, but it was only Humphrey Williams. She had noticed that his car was parked immediately beside hers, but had hoped, if she was quick, to be gone before he appeared. Now here he was, sidling down the too narrow space that he had left between them. For a moment she saw him clearly: his moist pink head, his kindly smile, the damp patches beneath his arms that the heat had made enormous; and then he swam out of focus as he bore solidly down upon her. She knew she was trapped before him, for the cars stood with their radiators almost touching the wall.

She clenched her fists. During her breakdown, physical contact of any kind had been completely unbearable, and she was still distressed by the way the symptom seemed to have lingered on. Today, with the heavy air pressing all about her, she knew she could not possibly endure the nearness of this large perspiring man. How could she stop him coming any closer? She would have to give him something else to do.

She held her bag out at arm's length, flapping it wildly up and down before him.

"I've mislaid my keys!" she said. Her voice sounded high and unnatural,.and she paused, making an effort to compose herself.

"Would you look in here for me?" she went on. "I'm in such a hurry, and I can't see very well without my other glasses."

He took the bag eagerly, holding it with care, as if he had been handed some delicate piece of porcelain.

Immediately she regretted her gesture. Why couldn't she have thought of another way to stop him? It was horribly intimate, standing beside a man while he fumbled through your handbag, especially here, under this wall. The skin at the base of her throat began to throb and tingle. In a moment the blush that plagued her would be rising, turning her neck and cheeks to scarlet before his watching eyes.

She tried to turn away, and in the constricted space her skirt brushed against the mudguard with a loud metalic click. Her keys! She must have put them in her pocket! The sensation of deliverance was so great that for an instant she quite forgot about Humphrey, and her face broke joyously into an unselfconscious smile. Now that the keys were found she would be able to leave immediately. She would have time to do the flowers properly after all.

Once, when she was young, her mother had told her that she should try to smile more often, remarking that the expression greatly improved her face. She had not believed her, for she felt that her pebble glasses had already put her beyond redemption, but for a time she had practised smiling as a sort of offering to Victor; anything was worth trying, if it might make her more pleasant for him to behold. It had not seemed to make any difference and she had forgotten about it, but by then the artificial smile had become a habit which she used on all social occasions. No one had ever told her again that a spontaneous flash of pleasure could transfigure her whole face.

Now she wondered why Humphrey was standing there silent, opening and closing his mouth in the manner of a fish. He certainly was most unattractive, but the impulse to recoil had left her now that the keys were back in her hands. It was absurd to be disconcerted by the way he always parked his car beside hers, or by the fact he sought her out in the staff room and the dining hall. It was hardly surprising, since they had much in common, their mutual interest in history and architecture, their love of the countryside.

"I'm very sorry," she said warmly, plucking her bag from his hand. "It was good of you to come and help me. I don't usually forget where I put things. It's all this thunder in the air."

She slipped the key into the lock as she spoke and picked up the plastic carrier. With the door ajar and her books in her arms, she felt completely restored to confidence.

"I can't imagine what you must think of me," she added apologetically. "I'm afraid I was in quite a state."

"Oh, not at all," said Humphrey quickly. "Not at all. That is, I mean to say . . . No! Not at all."

Usually she was irritated by the nervous way he repeated himself. It was ridiculously exaggerated; no wonder the children mimicked him, even to his face. But today her attention was diverted. The way he held the door open for her as she squeezed into the driving seat, the careful manner in which he shut it behind her as if she were too fragile, too precious, to withstand a slam, had reminded her forcibly of Victor. It was with just this same air of protective concern that he always said goodbye to Miriam. No doubt he had closed her door like this when she left for London on Wednesday – as if he had been seeing her off on a pilgrimage, and not an unnecessary spree. It almost made her angry to see the way he indulged her. No one else she knew would have been prepared for their wife to enjoy that sort of independence, gadding about all over the countryside, as Miriam liked to do. And this week, of all times, when there was so much to be arranged for the christening! He was far too good to her, too patient, too longsuffering. It was just as well that somebody was around to keep an eye on his household, since his wife seemed unable to undertake the job.

She turned the ignition on hastily and rolled up the window beside her. Humphrey had a tiresome habit of leaning with his elbows on the sill, and she absolutely must be on her way.

"Goodbye!" she cried, through the small gap that remained open. "Goodbye, and thanks again! Hope you have a good weekend."

As she backed out she saw that he was not to be shaken off so easily. He was limping doggedly along beside the car. She couldn't quite catch what he was saying, but there seemed to be a lot of laughter coming from all quarters of the car park. Perhaps it was directed at her? How she wished that Humphrey would not make her conspicuous before the rest of the staff! Embarrassment suffused her, misting up her glasses, making her hands slippery on the wheel, but she could not stop and wipe her lenses amid the ridicule of all these people.

She pressed her foot down hard on the accelerator and the car bounced forward, narrowly missing the gate post, and inserted itself, as if by magic, into a space on the busy road.

Driving was always an ordeal. For several months after her illness she had given it up altogether; but then it had been comparatively easy, for she had still been teaching at Frampton Hall. Living in, you can manage without your own transport, especially when your colleagues and friends are prepared to be helpful and kind. She remembered how Victor had come all the way up to Cambridge, and driven her home to see Father for the weekend; though not more than once or twice, as it was such a long distance, and he was naturally busy at Coombe.

Besides, at that time, Father had been extraordinarily

ungracious in his attitude; it was as if his grief over Mother's death had distorted his whole view of life. He seemed to think that Victor's marriage had been an insult to all of them, and had in some way contributed to her own breakdown; although that was clearly without foundation, for her involvement with Victor had started long ago, in childhood, and its nature had hardly changed. It was simply the fact that they were such close neighbours – and single, in a community where everyone else seemed to be married – that had caused their names to be casually linked together, and how could you blame Victor for that? Nor was it his fault if she had occasionally yielded to the lure of daydreaming, and allowed herself to imagine a different, more fulfilling relationship than the one they really enjoyed: that had been nothing but her own shameful foolishness, a humiliating weakness which she would rather forget. It was most unfortunate that Father's clouded mind had become fixed in the past, at a point where he had somehow penetrated one of those flights of fancy, and that he still attached such importance to the outdated memory – for of course it was years since she had even pretended to herself that Victor could be more than a close and affectionate companion; on the contrary, she had decided that he would probably never marry at all. He had shown himself impervious to the county's efforts to ensnare him, and she had ceased to feel surprise when she saw how difficult other women found him to talk to, and how blank was his response to flirtation and feminine guile.

It was quite out of character, it still struck her as astonishing, that he had picked out a girl as young and immature as Miriam, and fallen so completely for her obvious coquetry. She had heard that older men were often a prey to passionate infatuations, appearing almost bewitched, as Victor had done, but nonetheless she would have expected him to retain some powers of judgement. She only hoped his lack of them would not lead to unhappiness.

She clenched her hands on the wheel. It was intolerable to think that anyone might undervalue Victor's love, or hurt him in any manner, and just now she must not allow herself to contemplate such a thing. Any violent emotion, and most particularly anger, could ruin her concentration ever since her breakdown. The doctors had said that she must avoid undue stress and worry if she was to make a permanent recovery; and yet here she was, already distraught about something which would probably never happen, for surely not even Miriam, thoughtless and flighty though she might appear to others, could betray so consummate a trust?

Look! Here was the exit, and she had nearly missed it! But at least she had hardly noticed the most arduous part of the drive. The precious ten minutes were saved, and she would soon be safely off the motorway. It was absurd to think that she had almost gone cross-country to avoid the confusion and the noise. Now she would take the private road, where from Abbot's Bridge you could see Coombe Manor long before you reached it. She would not be put off by the fact that Miriam had also started to use the short cut; it was still her own particular and special approach.

As she passed through Hungerford the first huge drops of rain splashed loudly against the windscreen. They fell ponderously, one by one, as if an enormous tap had begun to drip above her, and she let them run down the dusty glass unheeded, not bothering to wipe them away. For she knew she could relax now, could stop straining her eyes to see where she was going. From here the car would carry her smoothly and confidently, as though guided by automatic pilot, following by habit the left turns and the right turns, twisting downhill between the narrow hedgerows, to where the final bend by the bridge at Abbot's Corner would offer her the first refreshing glimpse of Coombe.

4

"Watch it!" cried Miriam, though before her words were out she knew that Justin was already braking. She fell forward against her seat belt as the back wheels skidded and hissed between the narrow walls of the bridge. There was a crunch and a shock as the lurching bumper struck the stone work just behind her, and then incredibly they had stopped, almost touching the stationary car before them and the figure that crouched beside it on the road.

"All right?" said Justin tersely. He looked perfectly calm, but his face had gone a most peculiar colour. What a mercy he had been driving; she would never have stopped in time. He was trained to split-second reactions, and had not been showing off as she would have done approaching that well-known corner, hurling the car round it in the confidence that an uphill straight was round the bend.

"Fine . . ." she said, but he was out of the car before she could tell him how grateful she was for their deliverance, scraping the door on the confining walls that had so nearly been their undoing, and striding towards the woman who had scrambled to her feet. She recognised Dorothy and her car in the same uneasy moment, and opened her own door with determination, ashamed at her reflection of what the rain would do to her hair. What an idiotic thought, when Dorothy could have been killed, and when Justin was obviously going to tear the poor creature to pieces. She must rescue her immediately; what did it matter if the car had suffered a bit of a bang?

"For the love of God," Justin was shouting, "what made you stop in a place like this? On a blind bend? With a humpbacked bridge behind you? Have you gone crazy or something? Can't you see we could all have been killed?"

Dorothy was standing mutely, poised helplessly over her spare wheel and her puncture, and staring at him through the downpour as if she had seen a ghost. Water dripped from her face and hair, and her neat summer dress was sodden and streaked with oil and mudstains. She had grazed her knee too apparently, for her stocking was ragged with ladders and her leg was smeared with blood. There was something shocking, almost indecent, about finding Dorothy in such a state of disorder. It made her look ten years older – you felt you should turn away. But naturally that was impossible; Miriam advanced firmly and took her by the elbow. She tried to speak lightly and cheerfully to cover her dismay.

"It's all right," she said. "No harm done. Though thank God I wasn't driving! Don't pay any heed to Justin; he's had a shock, that's all. He'll change your wheel in a jiffy – come and sit in our car till he's finished. And for heaven's sake don't worry about it any more."

She guided Dorothy forward as she spoke, away from the picture on Justin's unfortunate T-shirt. It seemed to have mesmerised her in a curious manner, as if she was a rabbit confronted by a stoat. Or perhaps it was only his expression? Standing there in the cloudburst he did look amazingly satanic, and not unlike a skull himself, now she came to think of it, with his eyes so deeply set and his hollow cheeks beneath them, and his wet hair plastered down around the chiselled contours of his face. A sensational bone structure. But then Dorothy was in no state to appreciate its beauty . . . She pushed her hastily into the Volvo and went round to the driving seat.

"He won't be long," she said, "but I think I'd better reverse, so we're not sitting here on the corner. We don't want anyone else running into us from behind."

"No one else comes this way," said Dorothy loudly and shrilly. "It's a private road. It's part of the estate."

Miriam, starting the engine, looked round at her in astonishment. She sounded distinctly offended, as if some moral principle had been rudely and ignorantly contested, and yet behind her glasses you could see there were tears in her eyes.

Really, it was impossible to know what to do about Dorothy! She seemed to be getting odder and odder lately, and becoming quite unpleasant, though Victor denied that was true.

"Of course. You're quite right," she answered as soothingly as possible, but she backed the car round the corner, whether Dorothy liked it or not.

"The bridge wouldn't stand much traffic anyway," she went on conversationally. "Victor says the foundations are going. I know he means to get something done about it, but it's such an enormous job."

"He has too much to do," cried Dorothy, and her tone was brittle with indignation. "Far, far too much to handle. I don't know how he copes at all without anyone there to help him. I was going to do the flowers for the christening," her voice broke into a positive wail of anguish, "and now I'll hardly have time to get them started before Nurse Rose has got to go."

"Oh, for heaven's sake," interrupted Miriam sharply. "It doesn't matter in the slightest, we can easily manage to do the flowers ourselves." She paused, aware that she might have sounded ungracious.

"I mean, it was nice of you, of course, but you're not to fuss about it. Justin and I can always throw something reasonable together. As a matter of fact, Justin's usually an absolute wizard when it comes to flowers."

The remark was a mistake. She could tell that before she had finished speaking. Remarks about Justin invariably were a mistake, as soon as you found yourself back again at Coombe. They were followed by icy little silences and significant changes of subject; as were other unwise topics, like allusions to plays or the ballet, or music or poems you'd read. Though Dorothy had always been different, she did not fit into the mould of the Templeton image; in fact Miriam wondered quite often what it was that she found in them all.

For Dorothy was clever: she was skilled and successful in her profession. Victor said that, except for this breakdown, she'd have been a headmistress quite soon. Yet none of them wanted to observe her intelligence, it was just an embarrassment to them; it was lucky that her emotional dependence allowed everybody to patronise her comfortably without taking it into account. If the poor thing read a lot, it was probably because her job demanded it and everyone knew she must work to earn her living; and at least she had the good grace not to talk about it, except presumably to dear Victor who had gone through some peculiar phases himself when he was young . . .

Was it possible she did not care? Could it be that she did not notice that her brains and her job and her temperament made a gulf that she never could cross? Why, her background alone! Take her father now, old Bishop Buckley: Hester was fond of remarking that he'd certainly risen from nowhere, and made a good job of it too. And her mother, who came from 'some professional family in London' which no one, as Lizzie explained, had ever heard of . . . No, Dorothy was not true Templeton material. She might, for convenience sake, have originally shared their governess, but now she was more like a governess herself, retained out of habit although she was not really wanted; she was not by nature disposed to employ the heavy pause technique, or make use of the vacant stare.

That was why it was particularly upsetting to find her so stiff with disapproval this evening, and to see her recoil at the appearance of Justin, who was now, very kindly, attending to her tyre. However used Miriam was to this sort of reaction she had not expected it from Dorothy, and it certainly did not warm the heart. She stared back at her without affection; if Dorothy chose to be disagreeable then she regarded it as a pity, but she was perfectly prepared to follow suit.

"Just look at your clothes!" she began coldly. "They're absolutely soaking . . ."

She had been going to say 'so you'll have to go straight home and change them', but she bit the words short, arrested by the spasm of naked misery that contorted Dorothy's face. There was no mistaking its meaning, a child would have read her feelings without difficulty. 'My God,' she thought, 'it really matters to her! She's been looking forward to doing the things for days.' Her pain was grotesque, immoderate, out of all keeping with the trivial vexation that caused it, but it was real enough; it was clearly impossible to sit here and watch her endure it. Besides all this tension between them was weird, unhealthy; it was growing ugly and strangely alarming, it had got to be shattered at once.

"I know!" she burst out with a strained attempt at enthusiasm. "You can pop into something of mine while your dress gets dry. And surely Mrs Scott could do without Fanny for an hour or so this evening? I could easily run her over to Coombe Bassett when its time for Nurse to go."

There was a pause, and Miriam, peering through the misted windscreen, longed suddenly for a cigarette. The rain was slackening, but she could hear thunder grumbling in the distance as if foiled by the blanketing cloud, and though the first downpour was over, the respite was ominous and flagrantly deceptive, an empty and unnecessary truce. She drummed her fingers on the steering column. She wished that Dorothy's agitation did not communicate itself so easily, extinguishing her genuine pity with an irrational impulse to flee, it made this silence so difficult to contend with, though she felt she must give her a breathing space to get her emotions back under some sort of control.

"Fanny left last week," said Dorothy at last. "There's a new girl now – I'd have thought you'd remember that, Miriam. But you've got more interesting things to think of, I suppose."

Her voice sounded dull and exhausted and carried no flicker of friendship, but Miriam hardly noticed the absence of gratitude; it was such a relief to see that her lips were no longer trembling and the wild look had gone from her face. The hysteria or whatever it was that had threatened a moment ago was over, how absurd that she had let it make her nervous, that she had felt it to be hostile. She really must not start imagining silly things like that.

All the same, it was good to see Justin's wet face at the window, and she was glad when Dorothy completely ignored his offer to drive her car up to the house. She did not thank him either, but jumped out and squeezed herself hurriedly past the Volvo, scuttling up the road without looking behind her, like an animal released from a cage. With her dishevelled hair, and her ruined clothes clinging about her, she looked pathetically awkward and fussy, and Miriam stared after her unhappily, halfway between laughter and distress. It was awful that an ordinary wetting could strip so much away from Dorothy, as though the loss of her neat restrained appearance had made it impossible for her to behave in a conventional way. She hoped that a hairdryer and a clean dress would restore her, there was enough to attend to without devoting time and patience to pacifying the tantrums of Victor's peculiar friends.

"She's bats," remarked Justin laconically, settling in beside her. "Did you see the look she gave me? You'd think I'd been trying to rape her or something, instead of changing her cursed wheel!"

She had seen the look, but had made up her mind to forget it, and she rounded on him irritably, resentful at hearing him voice the thoughts she had carefully put away.

"Oh for goodness sake!" she said. "She's just in a flap, and she's always been a bit odd anyway. Let's get out of here, and stop bothering about Dorothy. We're much later than I said we'd be, and I'm simply longing to get home."

Longing to get home. The words, brought out casually, lightly, as custom and habit dictated, had not been meant to carry any meaning; but she suddenly realised with a flash of unexpected pleasure, that this time they were actually true. She *was* longing to get home. She wanted to see the gates, the lake, the elegant winding avenue, and the house with its warm yellow stone and its air of secure serenity. Permanent. Dependable. And she wanted, she really wanted, to see Victor standing outside it: no one banished an unsavoury atmosphere as quickly as Victor could do.

She passed Dorothy on the straight, with her hand on the horn and a feeling of reckless confidence and satisfaction. Let Justin frown and ostentatiously buckle his seat belt; she felt inviolable at this moment, protected even from her own atrocious driving, as if Victor had cast a safety net around her from the threshold of their house. It was only important to reach him at once, while she was still consumed by desire to be beside him. She must get there before she remembered the frustrations and the irritations – now, when she was filled with nothing but the proper and suitable sensations, the wish to see her husband, to be reunited with her baby, and to find herself comfortably enfolded in the welcome of her home.

5

There was no window in the little cloakroom under the backstairs; the lightning was obliterated, it could not reach her there. Dorothy washed her hands meticulously, scrubbing each nail with exaggerated care, pressing back the cuticles one by one as she dried them on the roller towel behind the door. It was not until she was scouring round the basin with the floor cloth that she realised how very deliberately, how really unforgivably, she was wasting her time. The flowers were finished, as perfect and exquisite as she had intended despite the frenzy of haste in which she had begun to arrange them, and now she should be hurrying home to poor Father, who for an hour or more had been left to the mercies of a girl who knew nothing of his wants and disabilities. Besides the storm was getting worse every minute, and her goodbyes were still to be said. Hester and William had arrived; they would all have congregated by now and be drinking in the library. She must rouse herself and unlock the door this very instant, must cross the two halls, where the lamps were dim, and the lightning, flashing intermittently through the great arched window on the stairwell, seemed exceptionally piercingly white, stabbing your eyes like an instrument of torture, making even the most familiar objects appear sinister and bizarre.

She reached out and touched the coats that hung reassuringly around her: all Victor's coats, years of them, some of them unused now, but all of them consolingly familiar. The whole room, in fact, was redolent of Victor. His boots stood in rows beside the basin; riding boots, fishing boots, muddy looking wellingtons. His hats crowded on the pegs above her. Even the towel, which she noticed with tenderness was rather dirty, carried the smudges from his half-washed hands. Yet tonight it had been a mistake to break off and seek this refuge, it had shattered the impetus that had swept her through the challenge of the flower arrangements, had destroyed the unexpected confidence that had buoyed her up ever since the job had begun.

She must go at once; she would take some valium to calm her. It was true that she always felt this step was retrogressive, especially now her breakdown was so far behind her, but there were still times, and this was certainly one of them, when it appeared the only sensible thing to do. It had been a nerve-wracking, exhausting evening, encompassing such black moments of despair and such surprising peaks of satisfaction that she felt it had gone on for ever, that she had been transformed a dozen times since that frightful instant on the bridge, when already soaked and sick with disappointment, she had looked up and seen the Volvo screeching down on top of her. Worse still had been the distorted period that followed, when her perceptions had gone awry again, and when she had seen Miriam and Justin as if they were far away at the end of some narrow infinitely evil tunnel, where they moved like marionettes, tiny but menacing. It must have been nearly a year since she had last experienced that particular sensation, as if a telescope, with its wrong end turned towards her, was immovably clamped to her eye. The image it threw always left her distressed, her own personality in fragments; this evening, for instance, when Miriam had passed her on the road, sounding her horn so loudly, waving her hand so gaily, she had felt . . . no, she would not dwell upon what she had felt as she watched the Volvo speed carelessly on through the park. She had been unwell for a moment, that was all, suffering from a fleeting insignificant relapse caused by the shock on the bridge: her thoughts at such times were not worthy of any scrutiny.

She took three pills from her bag and washed them down briskly. There was no point in doing things by halves, it was the decision itself that had to be treated with circumspection; once made she might as well enjoy the rare indulgence to the full. She was even tempted to wait here until the valium began to work a little, so she would feel less selfconscious as she entered the library, wearing Miriam's extravagantly fashionable clothes. But she must not be so foolish, it was only Hester and William who would be astonished, since she could hardly begin to explain to them that it was not her own garments she wore.

She glanced down at her skirt, bright colours splashed out at random over an inky background, a gypsy skirt, much longer than she would usually have thought of wearing, swinging round her legs in a flamboyant and ridiculous way; and the silk shirt, dark and brilliant as a garnet, that toned mysteriously with some dominant hue in the jumble of colours below, but that tended to cling to her body in an unpleasantly revealing fashion. She felt grotesque. Yet she could not help recalling that during the evening she had experienced an extraordinary thrill at being so oddly, excitingly clad. Even balanced on the stepladder by the pedestals in the drawing-room, she had felt neither awkward nor exposed nor dizzy, but had swirled her skirts joyously around her, extending her arms with the wide batwing sleeves that Miriam had assured her everyone was wearing, to receive the handfuls of blossom that Justin proffered to her from below. She had felt she was accepting a series of bouquets, and that Victor, passing occasionally beneath her, was applauding her performance in a way he had never done before. It had been wonderful, unreal, liberating; she had travelled a world away from the Dorothy who had shivered and dripped on Abbot's Bridge at the lost beginnings of the evening, and yet now . . . yet now she was abruptly back where she started, and on top of it all, attired in fancy dress.

They were all in the library when she finally made her entrance. William and his sons, with drinks in their hands, stood grouped around one of the long uncurtained windows, talking to Victor and watching the storm with an offhand bored politeness, as if Coombe had provided an unnecessary pantomine with which to welcome them in. Justin sat apart, thumbing through a pile of gramophone records, but he rose to his feet with surprising courtesy as she hesitated beside the door. His perfect face, the supple way he moved, the amusing sense of occasion that had made, she had to admit it, a festival of their mutual flower arranging – it was hard to dislike Justin quite as much as she felt she should, though his position as Jamie's Godfather was shockingly unsuitable. Victor had told her, with a lot of evasion and embarrassment, that the poor boy was a homosexual, and though it had eased her mind considerably about his relationship with Miriam, she felt that Victor should have reacted more firmly against his involvement with his son.

She smiled at him none the less, still warmed by his gallantry at the foot of the stepladder, and advanced doubtfully upon Hester who was sitting with Miriam beside the fire. Looking at them, it was hard to believe that it was Miriam who lived here, and that Hester, so wholly at home in this room that she seemed part of the sofa she sat on, was now the visitor.

From childhood they had all looked up to Hester, not only because she was the eldest, but because she was both implacable and domineering, the most capable, the least vulnerable of them all. Sometimes Jamie, a year or two younger, had dared to flout or contradict her, but then Hester had always been a little less confident with Jamie, as if disheartened by the fact that he would one day come into the inheritance for which she was so superbly designed and fitted, just because some bitter freak of fortune had made her a girl. Perhaps that had increased her determination to subjugate Victor and Lizzie who obligingly offered her no resistance – until, of course, Victor had come up with his stunning determination to marry Miriam, disregarding all advice, remonstrance and disapproval as if he had been stricken deaf. It must have been terrible for Hester; she had lived in London since her marriage, and had always considered and used Coombe exactly as a second home. They had come down almost every weekend, and the boys had spent months here in the summer holidays; and on top of that, though it was never mentioned, it had been perfectly clear that Edward was expected to inherit. He was already half way through an estate management course at Cirencester when Miriam's baby was born.

Now, as she approached Hester, it struck Dorothy that she had not seen her at Coombe all summer, and the thought that she had hardly noticed this unprecedented absence made her feel as flustered and guilty as if she had caused it herself. It was a new experience to feel sorry for Hester, but she realised at once that she could not humiliate her with tactless expressions of pity. On the other hand, it was surely out of the question to behave as if she had been meeting her on and off as usual? It was all dreadfully uncomfortable and confusing; her face was flaming as she bent down and kissed the handsome, casually presented cheek.

"How lovely to see you, Hester!" she cried, hoping her tone conveyed lighthearted pleasure. "What on earth have you all been getting up to in London? It seems such an age since we saw you down this way."

Hester jerked up her chin, and her nostrils dilated slightly. Dorothy was familiar with that expression, and knew at once that her jocular manner had been horribly ill chosen; she was also, and most undesirably, reminded of a childish remark of Miriam's – that Hester looked like a horse that could not get free from its nose bag. It was awful how Miriam's rudeness could imprint itself on your mind.

"We were down in May," Hester was saying acidly. "Just before the heatwave became really unbearable in London. But we didn't spend the night, and it was term time, that's why you didn't see us. Miriam had only asked us to come to lunch."

Dorothy felt herself floundering in the awkward pause that followed. She had realised that Hester was resentful, but had never expected her to sound so openly aggrieved.

"Well, how fast the summer has gone!" she exclaimed; any nonsense would do to break the agonising silence. "And how much dear Hugo has grown since I saw him last! I expect they're all looking forward to the start of the hunting, aren't they? It's so hard to believe it's really the middle of October; only a few more weeks to go."

She broke off nervously, remembering Miriam's violent objection to the pursuit of all blood sports, and the insolent way she gave vent to her feelings about them. But luckily Hester was already speaking, in the same bleak offended tone.

"Oh, I don't expect we will get much hunting," she said. "Things have changed a bit – you must realise that, Dorothy. After all, we must none of us forget that Victor's got his own family to think of now."

"Oh, you won't forget that," interjected Miriam calmly. "Not while I'm around to remind you." She drew her feet up on the sofa and lit a cigarette. "Anyway," she went on, "I expect that Victor's told you that he is cutting down a lot on the stables? He was going to talk to William this weekend, about whether the boys would want to take away a couple of the hunters. It seems silly to keep on such a lot of horses – when they're not being used regularly, I mean."

Hester is no match for her, thought Dorothy suddenly; all her tactics are useless in face of this sort of response. Miriam's protected from her because she is completely indifferent to her feelings, she can't be wounded by her scorn or her dislike or her censure. She simply doesn't care.

She looked away quickly. Hester was obviously quite unprepared for the ultimatum about the horses and it was shameful to take any pleasure from seeing an old acquaintance so casually, bloodlessly vanquished. Was it only the valium that made her feel like applauding? Or was it something to do with the last obscurely critical remark that Hester had made? Well, thank goodness here was Victor, urging a sherry bottle upon her: she felt almost tempted to accept some, though she knew that on top of tranquillisers it could make her feel extremely odd. But Father was waiting and the whole long process of getting him to bed still lay before her, not to mention a drive through the storm, which was now overhead to judge by the sensational crack of thunder and the flash that followed so swiftly. In the searing light she caught a glimpse of Justin, with his arm instinctively thrown up to shield his forehead, and for some reason the sight of his nervousness strengthened her: Victor would never, and she must not, behave in such a way.

"No, I won't have a drinkie," she said brightly. "No

drinking and driving in thunderstorms. Why Victor, it's naughty to press me! And besides just look at the time! I really must take myself home to poor Father. Duty calls!"

She turned round and waved a hand skittishly at the others. "Goodnight, everyone. I'll see you all tomorrow."

William nodded and smiled at her vaguely, and Miriam thanked her again from her nest of sofa cushions, but Victor took her arm protectively and ushered her towards the door. She glanced at him anxiously. Did he know how the words gushed out, absurd and affected, before she could stop them from coming? Did he think she was as coy and idiotic as she had sounded a moment ago? He had never heard her teach, or deliver a lecture; he had never, so far as she knew, even read her *Pathways to Comprehension*, for which, in those first halcyon years at Frampton, she had been so widely acclaimed. In the past such omissions had scarcely seemed to matter, she had been so completely at ease with Victor, had never felt herself forced or threatened in any way: but all that was gone now, as if somewhere in the throes of her illness she had lost the key to the simple communion that had been so important. Did he realise now, for instance, how much she longed to remain beside him, to accept a drink, to stay on and go in to dinner, to make this discordant evening a little easier for him to bear? How she hoped that he did! She had been so touched and flattered earlier on, when he had asked her to help him keep the peace tomorrow. Of course, he hadn't put it quite like that, but he had said enough to indicate that he needed her and relied upon her as much as ever. It was essential that she came up to his expectations of her, so that he knew he could always count on her to support him whatever mistakes he had made.

"Would you like me to come with you?" he was saying. He had found an umbrella from somewhere, and was shaking the dust out of its folds. "The new girl took the Mini, so I could come straight back again with her. It wouldn't be any trouble." But he glanced round as the gong sounded, strident and commanding through the hallway, and she defiantly shook her head.

"I'll be fine on my own. Good lord, it's no distance!" Did she wish that he would insist, prepared for her sake to be late going in to dinner? But no, that would be ridiculous: it *was* no distance down to Coombe Bassett, and anyway it was Victor who needed someone to look after him this weekend. It was much better that he should be ushering her out cheerfully, confident that she could deal with the dark and the tumult of rain and thunder – as if, in fact, he had never doubted what a sensible person she was.

She felt sure it must be very good for her, to be treated without allowance for her recent illness. She needed to build up her self-confidence and feel herself normal and capable again. An endogenous depressive. A manic-depressive psychotic. It was terrible to find yourself classified in such an ugly demoralising way. It was probably fortunate, on that head alone, that she had not stayed on at Frampton, where the stigma of her breakdown would have clung to her, for ever labelling her as a freak – an object, no doubt, of the sympathy and understanding she so often and childishly yearned for, but a freak, a curiosity none the less. At least Father, despite his strange notions about what was best for her, did not regard her as a curiosity, and it was marvellous to see that Victor had already forgotten the embarrassing way that her illness had made her afraid of the dark. She felt sure it was his faith in her common sense that was making the journey so easy. She was nearly home already, and only when crossing the bridge, where the uproar from the rising river had been deafening, had she felt in the slightest afraid.

She expelled her breath in a long sigh as the car rolled into the garage. At last! She was home and the lightning could no longer reach her. She leant back against the headrest and luxuriously closed her eyes. It was peaceful here, where no catastrophe could befall her, no demands be made upon her, but she knew that the longer she sat like this, relaxed and torpid, the harder it would be to rouse herself to cope with the rest of the day. She was going to get wet again too; it was a pity that Victor had forgotten to lend her the umbrella, but she would just have to make a dash for it through the rain.

She almost bumped into the car by the door. It did not look like a mini, she supposed Victor must have been mistaken, but she got herself into the hall somehow with the bag of books clutched against Miriam's silken shirt front, and her hair blowing untidily across her face. There were letters upon the table and she glanced at them apprehensively, unable to see clearly through the raindrops on her glasses. Could one be from Gaston Abbey? The top one, at least, was undoubtedly from Aunt Maud.

She was just going to pick them up when she heard a voice speaking quite steadily from the direction of Father's study, and she froze with her hand still extended, all regard for the letters abruptly swept aside. A man's voice, but the cadence was smooth and it certainly could not be Father's. He was hesitant, tremulous these days, ever since he had suffered his stroke: but this voice was quite different, beautifully modulated and controlled. It was strange that it was neither frightening nor jarring, despite its unexpected intrusion in her house.

She tiptoed along the passage and paused by the open door. Who was there, reading – for she knew now that he was reading – in that deep confident timbre, unrecognised and yet curiously familiar? She wanted to know, yet the voice was commanding, it did not encourage interruption: she leant her head against the embrasure and surrendered herself to the magic of the words

> "Although I do not hope to turn again
> Although I do not hope
> Although I do not hope to turn
> Wavering between the profit and the loss"

As she did not hope. But hearing the rhythm, the resonance, the hopelessness was less terrible, less lonely. What could she turn to, anyway? To herself? To Father? To Victor? To the nightmare of seething unresponsive adolescents who abused the gift that was all she had to offer? To the bottomless misery that was blazed daily before her understanding: the wars, the disasters and the famine, the children orphaned, diseased, broken before they could become whole?

She swept off her glasses, squeezing her eyes up to control the tears that rose helplessly, mawkish and unbidden. Dear God, who was reading this thing? Offering these words, so famous, so often repeated, in a way that carried a solace to her overwhelming emptiness? She could, she would, she might still reach up to it, seek comfort from the holy mother, the spirit of the garden . . .

> "Suffer us not to mock ourselves with falsehood
> Teach us to care and not to care
> Teach us to sit still"

To mock ourselves with falsehood. With what falsehood? With what did she mock herself? Something was there, some message for her, for the Dorothy who wandered, abysmally misdirected, following a compass that no longer pointed north: who was labelled obscenely inadequate, a disaster, an affective psychotic.

> "And even among these rocks
> Sister, mother
> And spirit of the river, spirit of the sea,
> Suffer me not to be separated
> And let my cry come unto Thee."

She slumped against the jamb of the door. It was over. Over. The exquisite powerful voice had offered its comfort and was finished. And the door, with a bathos that did not escape her, swung suddenly open as her weight fell upon it, leaving her exposed on the threshold to a blurred and indistinct interior and two people whom she could not see properly. She put up her hand, trembling, and clamped her spectacles back in position. There, immediately, was Father before her, and astonishingly there also was Humphrey, scrambling in his usual ungainly manner out of her own armchair.

She stared at him for a long instant, dazed and fuddled with incomprehension. Where had the voice that had riven and thrilled her come from? It was ludicrous to suppose that it had issued from Humphrey, from the Humphrey who stammered and quavered and, by his absurd hesitations and repetitions, reduced every sentiment to the banal. It was unbelievable that he could read poetry with compelling and charismatic authority. Yet there was no one else here, and the book that had slithered from his knee and lay spine upwards on the carpet was undoubtedly her own *Selected Works of Eliot*. Even his acute confusion underlined the fact that he had been caught out reading aloud, and reading aloud to himself moreover, for Father was peacefully sleeping on the other side of the fire. However incongruous it might seem, she must accept that the voice that had stirred her could only belong to Humphrey.

"But it's incredible!" she burst out spontaneously. "I would never have thought it possible for you to read that!"

She drew in her breath sharply, appalled at her indiscretion. How could she have said such a thing to Humphrey, betraying not only a rude amazement at his achievement, but the fact that she had eavesdropped shamelessly upon his privacy: and, in some ways most agitating of all, had shared with him an experience that was moving to them both? It was all very regrettable, and besides she felt suddenly abused and cheated, as if Humphrey had disguised himself in order to deceive her, exposing her, under false pretences, to a farcical and undignified rush of emotion that was making her look a fool. In any case, what had brought him here to see her? He must not be encouraged to pay unwanted calls.

She drew herself up, there were plenty of cutting phrases to deal with that kind of aggravation: after all, she had not learned to discipline whole classes of children for nothing. She must fix her eyes on a spot somewhere just beyond, just above Humphrey, and administer calmly a simple but crushing rebuke.

As she threw back her head, gazing icily into the distance, she found herself staring straight into Mother's attractively gilded looking-glass. There, framed by its cherubs and twisted garlands, was a figure that staggered her completely, a figure of no known identity, but who was far removed from the neatly clad sensible schoolmistress who was on the point of asserting her control. The woman she saw looked demented, her face was flushed, her glasses crooked, her hair in disarray. The wine red blouse she wore was splashed with raindrops, and where it was wet it was clinging and nearly transparent, disclosing not only the contours of her breasts beneath it, but actually outlining, almost as if she were naked, the shape of her nipples as well. It was shocking, not only deranged, but disgustingly immodest. As she glared at it horrified, she saw her own shame and inadequacy flood into the creature's expression and bounce back at her cruelly, crazily from the surface of the glass. This was how she appeared, her unworthiness accurately reflected. She wanted to blot it out, disown it, but instead she stood motionless, paralysed by an abrupt and bewildering dislocation, as if she had lost the ability to drop her eyes.

Humphrey moved then. He moved, by some blessed accident in the only direction that could possibly have released her: to the left, to the foreground, materialising, large and substantial, between her and the shattering face. And his voice, with its ordinary tone and familiar stutter, cut a path through the desolation, brought her back to herself, to the room, to the objects around her, freed her arms to grab frenziedly at the damp folds of her shirt front and tear them away from her breasts.

"Why Dorothy!" Humphrey was saying. "I'm s-so sorry. So very sorry. I've . . . I've startled you, I can see it."

He broke off, staring wonderingly at her for a moment. "You look different," he added. "Quite different. That's a really magnificent dress."

How ridiculous he was! Yet that last remark, thrown out impulsively and without hesitation, carried something in it of the other Humphrey, whose voice was filled with confidence and whose manner carried conviction, but only, it seemed, when he was sure he was alone. Besides his astonishment was too genuine to be impertinent: just so had she blurted out her feelings about his recitation, before propriety or reserve could qualify them and blunt their sincerity.

"Do you think so?" she ventured uncertainly.

She paused, pleased and surprised at how level her own voice sounded. "They're only borrowed plumes," she added with more asperity, "and a great deal too exotic for my taste."

"Too exotic?" said Father crossly, jerking suddenly awake. "I would never call it exotic, Dorothy. It is startling, remarkable poetry, and I certainly don't dispute it, but the word 'exotic' is entirely inappropriate. It does not describe it at all."

He had fallen forward perilously as he spoke and she hastened to rescue and rearrange him, but he struggled against her with feeble impatience, determined to hold the floor.

"This young man of yours –" he waved towards the spot where Humphrey had been sitting, "has been with me for hours, and has read to me very delightfully. And I think you should get him a drink and stop fiddling round with my cushions. He's been waiting to see you for quite long enough as it is."

Dorothy patted his hand. She had noticed before how the blackest moments, when they passed, often left her in this curiously elevated condition, as though she was punch drunk, her sensitivity dulled by the violence of her experience and then by its abrupt relief. To hear Humphrey – stout, bald as an egg, and well advanced into middle age, described as 'this young man of yours' might at other times have proved the grossest of embarrassments, but just now she felt capable of enduring anything that Father might say; she even found herself glancing over her shoulder, inviting Humphrey himself to share the joke. But unfortunately Humphrey was not smiling: he was shifting from leg to leg in apparent agitation, and peering unhappily at his watch.

"I'll have to go," he broke out. "I'd no idea how late . . .

How quickly time was passing. I was on my way back to Swindon and I just looked in", he turned stiffly towards her, "to see if you'd like to come to the theatre tomorrow evening. They're putting a very good show together over at Salisbury . . . and I thought . . . I mean, I really think you'd enjoy it. So I wondered if you . . .? I did try to ask you about it in the car park. But you seemed in such a hurry, and I don't think you caught what I said."

His voice petered out. His large face was perspiring again, and he had encountered a lot of problems in pronouncing his 'thought' and his 'theatre'. It seemed to Dorothy that an eternity had passed since he started to speak. But before she could answer, Father, now fairly beaming with enthusiasm, had intervened again.

"That sounds splendid!" he cried, brandishing his stick in their direction. "Off you go now, at once, the pair of you. You'll be late, as you say, if you hang around here any longer.

"There's a girl in the kitchen," he added confidentially to Dorothy. "I don't know where she came from, but she can easily put me to bed." He smiled up at her triumphantly. "Nothing to worry about, you see! You just go out and enjoy yourself!"

"It's not tonight, Father," said Dorothy loudly. "Humphrey's been talking about taking – about going to a play *tomorrow* evening." She had been going to say 'taking me out' but the phrase would only have been ridiculous, in the same league, or very nearly, as describing him as her young man.

"And I can't come tomorrow," she went on, turning to Humphrey. "I'm going to a christening in the morning, and there's a lunch party afterwards. I'll be much too tired to go out anywhere in the evening, and besides there's no knowing what time I'll get away."

It was such a relief to slip out of it so easily, so truthfully. Even Father could scarcely upbraid her, when she had such an excellent excuse. As she spoke she could see the prospect of the day unfold before her clearly, bright with Victor's appreciation of her moral support and tactful intervention, and crowned with her own delight in becoming Godmother to his son. Miriam, in this context, was essentially insignificant, and the other Godmother she had chosen was touring in the provinces somewhere, and couldn't come. There could be no dispute that it was her right, as well as her pleasure, to carry Victor's child in the church tomorrow when he was brought to be baptised.

She had got Humphrey as far as the hall now, though she had not really listened to what he had said on the way. It was hard to concentrate upon him properly when the prospect before her was so engrossing, but she must try to be more attentive, and respond politely to him before he went out. He was telling her about his youth club and how important it was that no temptation should come between him and his duty to the boys: they must be able to rely on him completely, and be confident that he would never let them down. It was good of him, she had to admit, to give so much time to a cause that must be daunting and difficult rather than rewarding; even brave of him, when you thought about his stammer and the taunts and mockery that it often brought down upon him at school.

Contrite, she picked up his mackintosh and held it out towards him, forgetting for a moment how unpleasant such garments had always appeared to her touch. Tonight, Humphrey's old coat was wet, and the wetness had brought out a curiously personal aroma, so that even with her eyes shut she would have known at once that it belonged to him. It was very distasteful. As she thrust the thing hastily in his direction, she was suddenly wracked by a shudder that no conscious effort could possibly repress. She felt almost as shocked, almost as disgusted, as if she had briefly swept Humphrey himself into her arms, and at the same time she was filled with a bitter and irritable resentment. Why did she find it impossible to relate to any man, however innocent the circumstances, with the pleasant easy response she could offer to Victor and to Father? She was getting old, and age should at least have made it easier to form undemanding attachments to other people, yet still she shrank from friendship, freely offered, as if it was an assault upon her person, as if she was still the gauche and fastidious schoolgirl she had been so long ago. She could not escape the fact that Humphrey's coat, his physical nearness, even the heavy night that bore jointly down upon them, were filling her now with panic and revulsion; and although it was not his fault, her impatience with herself spilled over to include him, and she found herself bundling him rudely out of the house.

He would not return to it either, she could tell that from experience. There was always a point, and it came quite soon in these fragile tentative relationships, when she went too far, when her fear and distaste became thoroughly offensive. No friendship, it seemed, could survive that moment and continue to deepen; not even a friendship as free from romantic attachment as this one with Humphrey had been. It made no difference that he had probably neither wanted nor contemplated any physical bond between them: if anything, that would make him even less ready to forgive her for finding him positively repulsive, for shuddering at the touch of his clothing, for exhibiting hysteria when he brushed against her side. She had seen the astonishment on his face, and she knew that surprise would soon turn into outrage, and that it would finally settle into a cold determination not to expose himself again to such an absurd indignity. No one, however undemanding and modest, was prepared to be looked upon as an object of disgust.

No, Humphrey would not be back. She herself had ensured that he would never read aloud again, to her, or to Father. 'Because I cannot drink there, where trees flower, and springs flow, for there is nothing again . . .'

As she heard the car door slam she bent forward a little, clasping her arms protectively across the knot in her stomach. It was foolish, it might even be harmful, to allow herself to become so upset. She must look on the whole thing sensibly – the incident, after all, was trivial; she had long ago come to terms with her inhibitions, it was not as if she had expected to find any improvement or change. She was sorry, of course, that she had offended Humphrey, but at least after this he would disturb and fluster her no longer, and that could be nothing except an enormous relief. An enormous relief. She would see it like that in a moment. It was only a matter of keeping herself completely calm.

She stood very still by the door as Humphrey's engine choked and spluttered reluctantly into life on the other side of the panel, and her nails dug painfully into the flesh above her elbows as she heard the car driving away.

6

Miriam walked along the landing irresolutely and stood for a long time with her hand on the knob of the nursery door. She had already been in, several times, to see the baby; she had smiled over him with Victor, displayed him proudly to Justin, allowed Dorothy to hold him. She had listened, with the rapt expression she reserved for such moments, to Nanny's interminable catalogue of the minutiae of the last three days; and finally, because Victor insisted it was every parent's duty, she had gone upstairs with him again at drinks time, so that they could 'pop in' together and say goodnight. In fact she was already growing heartily sick of the very idea of babies, and of the claustrophobic cult that seemed to surround all nurseries she had ever known. The thought of Lizzie arriving tomorrow gushing and obsessive, with her own four children at her side, did nothing to alleviate her feelings. Lizzie would profess enchantment, would nurse and cuddle and croon over Jamie, until, in the vast indiscriminate mantle of her maternal urges, he became simply the quintessence of all babies, devoid of the subtle touching traces of character that made him uniquely her own.

She ran her hand through her hair, pulling angrily at the complicated new tangle of curls she had acquired with such enthusiasm. Why should she object if Lizzie, or anyone else, reduced her baby to this amorphous level, when that was exactly where she wanted him to be? Why else had she engaged a professional nurse to tend him? Why else had she weaned him abruptly and escaped as fast as she could? Only because she was determined to break the bond that had roused her to such a state of frantic misgiving; because she wanted to see him precisely as Lizzie saw him – a delightful adjunct to life, part toy, part talking point, part triumphant achievement: and of course an essential outcome of a proper marriage to Victor, a symbol of her worthiness as a woman and as a wife. Yes, that was undoubtedly the part that she had designed for Jamie, and she should be glad that this weekend might make it easier for her to relinquish him completely to the role she had created him to fill.

There must be no backsliding. She must not give herself any opportunity to rediscover the demanding personality beneath the surface whose hold on her had been growing at such an alarming rate. If she was not careful she would be caught again, and stifled in another intimate and complicated relationship, from which she could never hope to be free. It was bad enough, surely, to feel responsible for both Mother and Dickie, to have worried and grieved for them year after punishing year? And on top of that there was Justin, who had cherished her when her world had collapsed around her, and who now seemed joined to her in some mysterious manner, as if they had been fused permanently together by the trauma of those early bewildering days.

It seemed no time ago, and yet she had been very young then; no more than sixteen when all Dickie's frauds were discovered, and only seventeen when he had finally been sent to jail. Dad's pretty wilful little girl, whom he spoilt and indulged with an almost desperate generosity, so that even as a child she had known that his giving was suspect, had sensed that it was prompted as much by guilt and contrition as by ordinary fatherly love. She had used that knowledge too, and played upon it unmercifully, confident that he would deny her nothing in his efforts to compensate her for the lack of affection in her home. And yet, in the end, it had not been the loss of Dad the Provider that had mattered. She had not cared much when he told her that he was in money difficulties, that the wild extravagances were over, that the house, and the yacht and the holiday villa would have to be sold to pay off the most pressing of his debts. She had not really minded either when she found out that things were much worse than he had admitted; that his cunning speculations had misfired in a sensational manner, and that the money 'borrowed' and lost in an attempt to save his interests had been raised in an illegal way. She had never thought of Dickie as particularly honest; in fact all his better qualities, his exuberance, his charity, his zest for living all seemed inseparable from his dubious attitude to business, from the way he revelled in risky deals and knife-edged gambles, and cheerfully and profitably guided himself through the mess. 'Sailing close to the wind' was how he described it, and she had never blamed him, rather she had admired him for it, and for the relish with which he steered his cocky disreputable boat. If he had ended up by capsizing, then to her it was purely a financial disaster; she had not condemned him before, and she could see no moral difference between failure and success.

No, it was not Dad's dishonesty that had shocked her, nor the shame of the public scandal, nor her mother's vindictive bitterness. She was used to all that; she had learned to acknowledge and then to ignore it. It was Dickie himself, his complete and devastating collapse as a person, that had rocked the foundations of her stability. It was inconceivable that the Dickie she knew should disintegrate in such a manner, alternately cursing and cringing, crying vengeance and begging forgiveness, drinking, weeping and exhibiting himself before both friends and enemies as a creature devoid of courage or staying power or pride. She had never known before how much she relied on his massive self-confidence, how completely she had trusted his judgement and his values, his ability to look after her in the face of all possible odds. Bereft of his backing, and confronted by the pathetic failure that had replaced it, she had lost the only security she had ever known. If it hadn't been for Justin, for Justin's compassion and tenderness and admiration, she did not know, even now, how she would have found the strength to survive. He had hauled her along in his wake, enthusing, cajoling, sometimes hectoring. He had sat with her in the courts, visited Mother at the hospital; he had encouraged her through drama school, supported her in her ambitions. He had comprehended her loneliness and her confusion and had set himself out to conquer them as if they were his own. Life without Justin then was simply unimaginable. It was not until she was dazzled by the first blaze of Victor's adoration that she had really believed that she would ever be whole and independent again, or discover a means to make the break. It was terrible now to be a prey to these moments of doubt and desperation, when life without Justin seemed suddenly no more imaginable than it had ever been.

She turned from the door, dropping the cold brass handle as if it had burned her. She would not go in to Jamie. She would keep her distance and he would remain an enchanting plaything for her to enjoy. She had done with exposing herself to torment and disappointment. She had more than enough to contend with as it was. She must be mad to stand here, moonstruck before the nursery door as if she was playing the part of a disconsolate lover.

She gazed irritably down the deserted passage, seeking diversion from outstaring the portraits that hung upon the walls. They were indifferent portraits anyway, and most of them needed cleaning; all the better paintings were enshrined in the rooms below. Here were aunts and uncles only, and cousins and distant connections, though it was odd to see how the family resemblance united them. Hester's nose was certainly predominant, endowing them all with the same lofty superior stare. Well, she'd given them Jamie to add to the collection. She had borne him to be another Templeton, not as an extension of herself but as a source of pride and satisfaction to his father. Thank goodness she had realised in time what a terrible pitfall the whole affair could be.

Though only just in time. It was frightening to remember how confident she had been in pregnancy, how unaware of the huge emotional trap she was digging day by day. There had been no shadow then, no presentiment that she might not find it easy to give up the baby – to surrender him entirely to his surroundings and watch abstractedly as he took his place in the tableau, growing up just as Victor wanted him to do. That had been the whole point of the venture, and as a bonus she knew she would seem more conventional when she had produced the heir Victor wanted. Baby talk would provide common ground where she would be welcomed as an equal, it would be her passport to a world of impenetrable doors.

It was not until her labour was over that the flaws in the plot had become apparent, not until they clustered round her as she lay back exhausted and pressed the baby upon her to hold. Then of course she had seen in a flash that the scheme was in danger of misfiring completely, had been based on a wrong assumption from the very start. For the baby was hers – her own, in a way for which nothing had prepared her. Her own to a degree that could make nonsense of such words as abstraction and freedom of mind. Her baby, born of her body: at that moment it hardly mattered that he was also Victor's. He was so completely a part of her that other claims on him were totally insignificant. As she had stared down at him in mingled ecstasy and horror, her one coherent thought was that he looked remarkably like poor Dad. . . .

Yes, it had been a gruesomely narrow escape. She pulled herself up sharply, nearly colliding with the banisters that surrounded the circular stairwell, rather shocked to realise that she had actually been running along the landing away from the nursery door. As she stood there, staring sightlessly through the dusty branches of the chandelier below her, a wave of yapping swept up to her from the hall. The dogs. It seemed very early for bed, but they were obviously letting the dogs out, the first and most important ritual of preparing for the night. She could hear their voices dimly above the shrill barks and eager whining; a commanding 'Down there!' from Hester and a 'Steady on, Jester!' in Victor's most hearty tone.

Had she always loathed dogs? Looking back, she didn't think so; or perhaps they had simply not impinged upon her? She was sure she had not objected to these ones particularly until she was living permanently at Coombe. Even now, she suspected that it was not the dogs themselves that had changed her disinterest into positive aversion; it was the attitude that everybody took towards them that made them so hard to bear. Alone, she could easily have coped with the inconvenience, have dismissed their hairs and smells as just another household hazard, like the inadequate plumbing, or the persistent draughts; but she could not overlook the maddening assumption that they were the pivot of everyone's attention, an absorbing topic for conversation and an indispensible feature of any normal life. One dog now – she could probably have grown attached to a solitary animal, look how dearly she prized their scruffy old tom cat, and how much she had minded surrendering him to Justin when she left the flat? But one dog did not fill the requirements, like only children they were totally out of fashion. It was a case of the more the merrier, a good pack to be walked and fed and whistled at and tripped over, or piled steaming into cars and brought to luncheon parties, where you could let them out from time to time and watch proudly as they drenched their new surroundings with urine. And those endless discussions about pedigree and breeding potential! These days they were making her feel positively ill, as if she was poisoned with boredom; yet they all took for granted that nothing was more engrossing than another tale about a mysteriously risky and uncertain coupling, or a disastrous litter fed hourly by fountain pen ... It was all quite inexplicable, the more so since she knew that they did not care for the dogs very deeply: perhaps that was the most offensive and astonishing thing of all. When one died it was quickly replaced, and not only in fact, but apparently in the affections, and the failures were weeded out remorselessly, there was no unnecessary mourning for the sheep worrier or the gun shy. She had noticed too that despite the foetid cars the wretched things would suddenly be left behind for months without compunction, banned from the house and shut up in the farmyard while the family were away from home. It would have been wholly unthinkable to treat Tom in such a way. She slapped her palm down viciously on the ballustrade, as if the sharp sting of the mahogany rail might bring her to her senses. Even if the obsession was bogus as well as boring, it was ridiculous to let it annoy her as much as it did. She would go down again, so that when they came in she could say goodnight politely.

As she turned towards the staircase her eye was caught by an unexpected glint of light at the far end of the east wing. Someone was up already and their door was ajar by the look of it. Now that the commotion had died away below her she could hear strains of music coming from that direction too. She moved towards it, listening. Stravinsky. She felt too edgy tonight, too frayed and irritable to want to listen to Stravinsky, but on the other hand Stravinsky could only mean Justin, and a bedtime chat with Justin might help her towards a less disgruntled frame of mind. Besides, this was the 'Rite of Spring', and it seemed to be nearly finished; maybe she could get him to put on a more soothing tape.

As she waited dutifully outside the door – it seemed heartless to interrupt as the Chosen Maiden was shirling into oblivion – she became aware that her new affliction, an acid bottomless ache that was quite foreign to her, was creeping stealthily over her again. It had been so severe, and at first so unexpected, that she had tried to explain it to Justin, afraid that perhaps the birth of the baby might have upset her metabolism and left her emotionally ill. But Justin had only shaken his head and looked at her in amazement. "That's just homesickness," he'd said. "Don't tell me you've never been homesick?" But she hadn't, she supposed, or at least not until now. With a little moral blackmail Dickie had dropped all thought of sending her to boarding school, and although his existence with Grace had not offered her any sort of domestic refuge, she had known instinctively that she belonged to London, and from London she had never been thrust apart.

Now on this elegant landing, in the house she had won for herself with such artful calculation, she found herself assailed with a biting loneliness. Perhaps it was simply the jolting effect of the music, for it was in this ballet, with its savage primitive impact, that she had first seen Justin dance. Of course, that was long ago, at the start of everything for them both. It was years before he began to get solo parts at all, longer still before he was finally made a principal. But to Miriam, in love at sixteen, he had instantly appeared to be flaming, no ordinary member of the Tribe but irrepressibly, dazzlingly different, unmistakably a rising star. And now it was back, washing over her, the glory of that evening. She could almost smell it, the grease paint and the sweat, the exhaustion, the intensity, the comradeship – why had she chosen to throw it all away? What was she doing here, playing the lady of the manor, surrounded by yapping dogs in a world she did not even wish to understand?

She went in without knocking and leant against the door as it clicked shut behind her. Justin lay sprawled on the bed with his feet on a pile of pillows, supporting a glass in one languidly graceful hand. How debauched he looked! Except that she knew Justin never drank alcohol under any provocation. The glass would contain only soda, or perhaps tonic water, and the pillows were just a concession to the welfare of his feet. His self-discipline was spartan, yet he always made the most mundane situations sensual, like shaving in the morning or stacking the dishes in the sink . . . Even after all this time the anomaly could strike her as engaging, and she found herself smiling at the sight of him and the characteristic way he had draped himself across the bed.

"Enjoying your orgy?" she said.

He did not start at the sound of her voice, or even turn his head in her direction, and instantly the feeling that she was expected rattled her. She did not like the thought that her loneliness was obvious, so obvious that Justin could sit here in his bedroom and blandly assume she would follow him upstairs. Still, it was too late now; the best she could do was express disapproval that he had escaped so early, she could hardly deflate him with an act of complete indifference since, after all, here she was.

"I hope you've not been rude to the others, have you?" she began severely. "What on earth brought you up here so quickly anyway?"

"Hunting." He took a sip from his glass and looked into it gravely, as if meditating the bouquet of the tonic water. "And also something particularly revolting, called clubbing, or was it cubbing? I didn't like to show my ignorance, but it was all to do with killing things down their burrows when they're trapped and can't get away.

"They won't have missed me," he continued. "I can cope with farming, and charity balls and how-to-occupy-the-children, but I'm just a dead loss in the tally-ho sort of conversation. I slipped out when they started swapping stories about some old maniac called Basher Montmorency. Seems he's a glorious legend in this part of the country, but I'm afraid he sounded the angelus for me."

He sat up suddenly and patted the bed beside him. "Come here and sit down," he said. "There's something I want to discuss with you quite badly."

He drew up his legs and clasped his arms loosely round them, watching her over his knees as he rocked slowly to and fro. Now that he was looking at her properly, she saw with surprise that he too was tense and wrought up about something, though she couldn't make out whether the casual pose was merely intended to hide the fact that he was excited, or whether he was also guilty and ill at ease. She kicked off her shoes and settled herself down opposite him with her back against the bedpost, stuffing one of his pillows between her spine and the twisted barley sugar stick of wood. It was all very pleasant and comfortable but she really must not stay here long, they'd all be coming up in a minute.

"Well, fire away!" she said.

Justin sighed, and she looked at him sharply, hoping that whatever was coming was not going to spoil the one contented moment of the day. He seemed to be having difficulty in getting started, though his first words, in contrast to his silence, were innocuous enough.

"I suppose you remember meeting Beverley Lomax?" he said.

"Oh, for heaven's sake!" she exclaimed.

It had been one of life's big moments, that evening with Beverley Lomax. For some years now he had been hailed as the most thrilling talent that ballet had seen in half a century, and although his position as the world's leading choreographer was still hotly contested, somehow the controversy that raged round him seemed to sharpen and enhance his glamour and keep his creativity at fever pitch. On top of all that, he spent so little time out of America – it had been astonishing enough to get a chance to meet him, let alone to find that he was really interested in Justin; had singled him out and talked with him earnestly for half the evening, encouraging and complimenting him to his face. Looking back she found that the scene, far from fading, had become almost piercingly vivid, as if it was picked out in psychedelic colours, more like a dream sequence than something completely real. It was insulting of Justin to ask her if she remembered such an extraordinary evening, especially one they had both mulled over for weeks on end.

"I'm not gaga yet," she said coldly. "I don't find my memory's at all affected by the country air . . ."

"All right, all right," he interrupted placatingly. "I'm sorry. He has just been back in London, that's the point. And this time, you will hardly believe it, he has made me the most amazing offer! He's asked me to go to the States with him, to work on a whole new series of his productions. He says my own roles would be central, that we'd create them between us, together . . ."

He paused, and she could feel him leaning forward, but she did not look up. Instead, she stared down at her hands where her fingers appeared to have locked rather painfully together, heavy with Victor's enormous family rings.

"I see," she brought out eventually. "And you're thinking . . . you're wondering whether to leave the company?"

He bounced back on the mattress, making the curtain rings above them rattle.

"I did wonder," he said. "But I've decided now. I'm going. I've told the company I won't be renewing contract – or not this time at any rate. They were very reasonable about it. They seemed pretty sure I'd want to come back one day, and that then they'd reap the benefit of everything he'd taught me. Anyway, they must know how cramped I've been starting to feel there lately; it's hard not to, with Michael and Tony around. Of course they're great, and I know that I'll get my chance when they are finished: but I need air *now*, new stimulation, even a little bit of glory. And just think of working like that with Beverley Lomax! My God – can't you see it? It's like a miracle! It's the chance of a lifetime for me."

He stopped expectantly, and the silence grew rapidly, spreading like a swamp between them, a living almost tangible thing.

What was the matter with her? She must scrape together some sort of enthusiasm, put on some sort of a show. She must congratulate him, and generously express her pleasure; tell him how much he deserved this opportunity and how wonderful it was. But the words were not there: it was worse than the worst first night, the script blasted from her memory and no prompter around to assist her. She would have to postpone the congratulations till Justin's words had settled, or at least stopped exploding like charges of gunpowder somewhere inside her head. Yet she couldn't get up and leave him without finding some way of answering.

"What will happen to Tom?" she faltered out at last.

"Oh, Miriam!" cried Justin, and for an instant his voice sounded rough with emotion, almost as if it was breaking, so that she feared her ridiculous remark had shown all too plainly how stunned she felt. Still, perhaps she was mistaken, for now he was hurrying on quite cheerfully, as if concern about a cat was a completely appropriate reaction to his sensational news.

"Tom should be all right," he was saying. "I've fixed up for Connie to keep him. He's been going up to her flat every day – oh, for a long time now. He was very lonely when you cleared out and left us, and she's grown really fond of him over the last year or so.

"I'll be selling the flat," he went on. "If I come back at all I want everything to be different. Besides, as usual, I'm broke.

Derek Lusk — you remember him? — he said I could move into his apartment till I'd time to get my bearings, but I know he'd find somewhere for me to rent instead if I asked him to look around."

He swung his legs off the bed, and went over and stood by the window, drawing back the curtain and peering out into the rain.

"I told him to wait until Monday," he said, barely looking over his shoulder. "I told him that after the weekend I'd have found out for sure about you."

"About me?" She stared at his set back wildly, and as he whipped round she could feel his vitality leaping out towards her as if he had come on stage for a difficult solo dance.

"About you," he repeated tersely. "About whether you wanted to throw up this extraordinary pageant and come to America with me." He paused, as though willing the urgency to die away around him. "Or not," he said.

There was something about those last words, about the casual offhand way in which he tossed them in her direction, that counteracted the glassy effect of the shock. How dare he speak like that, implying that both of them knew her experiment with Coombe to be a failure? Inferring that she might leave her husband and her son? Could he not see how well she had done for herself, that she had landed not only this beautiful house, but a dominant social position? That the Templetons were welcome, had been welcome for centuries, in houses grander still, scattered proudly through all the country from Land's End to John O'Groats? And that now she was welcome with them? Just what did he think he could offer her that she wanted? Did he think that his flight into stardom would make it easier than before? Did he think she wanted to see him flower, watch him working with Beverley Lomax, knowing all the time that she was nothing beside him, that whatever she did she would always be second rate? Small parts in bad plays, and long gaps in between them? Cheap clothes, cheap food, scrimping and saving to pay for the roof above their heads? Fatigue and bickering and piles of dirty washing, and those miles, those years of hard grey pavements stretching out before her all over again?

He was mad, contemptible, crazily conceited. She wanted to punish him for this insult, to hit back, to wound him, hurt him in some final obliterating way. Well, perhaps she could best do that by laughing, by showing she found his suggestion so pathetically wide of the mark that it was amusing rather than offensive.

"You're joking, I take it, Justin?" she said lightly, jumping off the bed in a brisk I've-got-to-go-now sort of manner. "Because if you're not, then we'd better forget the last part of this conversation. I'm sure you don't want me to think that you have gone out of your mind."

It sounded quite well, she thought, though the laugh at the end could have done with some rehearsal. She had wanted it to show that she could not conceal how funny she found his behaviour; but she had let it ring out a bit too stridently perhaps, sharper and less good humoured than a giggle ought to be.

None the less, she waited in confidence to find out what way her derision would affect him. Would it anger him or defeat him? Would he climb down and apologise to her at once?

She could hardly believe her eyes when she found that he was grinning; that he was practising some exercise or other with his hand on the back of a chair.

"Wow!" he exclaimed. "My goodness, darling! The country air may be healthy, but it's certainly done for your acting! If you want to get on in New York, you know, you'll have to do better than this."

She sprang at him then, unable to hold off any longer. It came to her, as she flung herself furiously against him, that of course that was what she had wanted to do all the time. To strike him, to hit him: but as he caught her by the wrists and held her out struggling like a clockwork doll in front of him, she knew that even that was less than true. What she wanted was to hold him, to cling to him for comfort: and she wanted him to make love to her, here, now, without letting her go. She was suddenly hollow with need of him, light-headed, shaky as if she had been fasting. She must have him again. She must feel him above her, inside her. She must savour once more the strength of his whole lithe body, hot and naked beneath her hands.

Her arms dropped to her sides with his fingers still fastened around them, and he pulled her instinctively towards him, almost lifting her off her feet. There were noises in the passage, she could hear a blurr of voices, the creak of footsteps passing, but they carried no more significance than if they were coming from another world. It was all far away, in abeyance, like the need for decision or parting . . . nothing mattered just now except Justin and the hunger that had to be fed. Only Justin was real; only Justin and the rapture of finding that they were back again together, soaring, drowning, cleaving desperately to one another, on the bed where only a moment ago they had seemed so immeasurably apart.

7

Victor lay on his back and stared upwards into the blackness. It was very dark, too dark to make out the comforting shape of the fourposter bed above him, or the silhouette of Mother's pretty chaise-longue that usually stood out clearly against the curtains behind. The darkness was so dense, in fact, that if it were not for Miriam's even breathing beside him, he could well have been back again in the cabin of his ship. It was horribly stuffy too, despite the high ceiling and the big open windows; since he had married and moved into his parents' bedroom, he could not remember a night as stifling and impenetrable as this.

He moved his legs fretfully searching for a cool patch. There was no doubt that the blanket was making him uncomfortably hot, and yet he had cast it off several times already, and without it he found himself shivering and chilled. He was hardly ever ill, but he supposed that a rising fever might account for this unaccustomed wakefulness and anxiety. He put an exploratory hand to his forehead and was almost disappointed to find it cool and dry – though of course, with tomorrow coming, it would be disastrous for him to feel off colour. Really, he didn't know what had come over him; he seemed to be looking at everything from a strangely perverted angle tonight.

Maybe that would explain the unhappy exchange he had had with Miriam? Looking back, it was easy to see that it might all have been his fault. It was true that he always sat and talked to her while she soaked in the bath, and that she herself had first encouraged the habit, but it was pointless to pretend that he had not known he was being shut out this evening: it had been in resentment, rather than affection, that he had followed her into the bathroom, inflamed by the deliberate significance with which she had closed the door. He had probably seemed intrusive and importunate, as if he couldn't leave her alone or respect her privacy – although never before had she been so petulant and jumpy, nor rejected him in such an off-hand and hurtful way. The whole episode was extraordinary, indeed if he had not been awake ever since he would have wondered had he dreamed it. After all, if she was out of sorts, he would only have soothed and pampered her. She must know he would never make love to her unless she was ready and willing: he never had. And yet, when he pointed that out . . .

He sat bolt upright suddenly, jerked like a puppet by the stabbing memory. That was the kernel of the worry. It was not the disharmony he had felt in his house all evening, nor the lowering weather, nor even Miriam's unusual lack of sexual response that had upset him; at least they had not upset him enough to be keeping him awake. It was only the recollection of one sentence, and the impression of hidden danger it had carried, that would not let him rest. It was as though he had stumbled abruptly into a game of Russian roulette: one wrong remark, one false move, anything that by chance or ineptitude had caused him to goad her further, and a hideous catastrophe might engulf them both.

He had never been given to fanciful comparisons, and the force with which this one struck him was alarming. Worse still, it was clear that the aura of nightmare was growing steadily stronger as the details began to fade. Perhaps, if he retraced the whole miserable conversation, it might bring him back to normality again?

All right, he would try it. What had he said as Miriam stood rigid and unyielding in the goodnight embrace he offered? Something inoffensive about realising that she was exhausted, he could not remember exactly how it had gone: but the phrase with which he had ended came back to him precisely.

"I would never ask anything of you unless it was just what you wanted." That was what he had said.

He would not have minded her laughing, would not even have minded her laughing *at* him, for it had always been good, whatever the reason, to hear Miriam laugh; but this time it had been different. She sounded derisive, mocking, as if she despised him and looked on his words with contempt.

"Oh Lord!" she had said. "Don't you think I already know that? You're so good that it makes my head ache just to look at you. It's like living with a bloody saint!"

The words had hurt of course, but he saw now that it was her expression that had shaken him so profoundly. Her whole face had looked quite different for a moment, as if it had grown sharper and narrower; infinitely colder, infinitely older than the girlishly innocent face of his wife: and as he stared at her, meeting with incredulity the eyes of a shrewd and indifferent stranger, he had experienced something else quite foreign to his nature, a foretaste of vengefulness so black and cruel that he was appalled to find himself still at its mercy. It was true that from the Miriam he worshipped he would never ask any sacrifice or demand any favour . . . but if she was a sham, if he found she had deceived and manipulated him, then by heaven she would find the price was crippling and, to the last farthing, he would make her pay . . .

He pressed his fingers to his eyes. This was lunacy, total lunacy. Where had these senseless evil feelings come from? What was happening to him? He must put a stop to such madness before it got a grip on him. He would get up, go downstairs, take a walk outside – anything to escape the suffocating muddle that had built up, inexplicably, in his own bedroom.

He moved stealthily towards his dressing room door. In any other house he would have been clumsy and noisy, bumping into furniture and knocking things down, but here at Coombe he was neat and sure footed as any nocturnal animal that hunts on its own territory. He had learnt by heart the pattern of creaking boards and scattered chairs that could betray him, for in childhood he had often crept across this room. In those days any blunder had meant complete disaster, for what could have been worse than those chilly scoldings in the night nursery, so far from the warm forbidden haven of his parents' bed? But that was long ago, and now his furtive movements were purely automatic; though as he closed the door he did wonder, for one brief uneasy moment, why his hands were damp and his heart pounding? Surely he was not frightened of waking up his wife? He had never worried about that, for Miriam always slipped back into sleep without any trouble. Could it be that he feared she might confirm the horrible fantasy he had woven in the dark?

He turned on the lamp, and at once the question was answered. All his doubt and anxiety receded in the light. It was just as he had hoped, the whole thing had been nothing but a monstrous aberration, and now it had vanished, exorcised by the wholesome ambience of his dressing room. He looked round him with satisfaction; already it was difficult to believe that he had reacted in such an exaggerated way. There was nothing wrong, no whirlpool in wait for him beneath the surface: his shoes, ranked formally on their wooden shoe trees; his brushes with their silver backs, lying where he had dropped them; Father's smoking jacket on the chair, a little frayed and threadbare but still serviceable thank goodness – everything told him so.

He breathed in deeply, absorbing the stale, almost musty smell that issued from the wardrobe. It was a good smell. Uncomplicated. Entirely and reassuringly male. It confirmed that nothing was changed, for he had never allowed women in here, with their open windows and sweet scented cleaning fluids. This was his province, exclusive and masculine, and no one was going to intrude upon it; not even, somehow particularly not, Miriam, with her curious habit of questioning the values of his life. It would be different with Jamie. One day, when he was grown, the boy would come in here and watch him changing for dinner, and he would encourage him to talk of school, or cricket, or hunting, just as his own father had done.

Almost reverently he picked up the circular ebony box that had held the trinkets of succeeding generations, and began to sort out the scatter of cuff links that lay on the dressing table, dropping them into it, two by two. These ones, small, gold, engraved with Grandfather's initials, they would do very well for Jamie. There was so much to plan for now. Old Molly, for instance, was about to foal at any minute; he had risked that again especially for his child. Wonderful blood. An excellent disposition. He would break the foal himself and school it to perfection so that it would be ready for his little boy to ride.

He turned on his heel. That was what he must do. He would slip down at once to the stables, see that Molly was calm and comfortable and had not been disturbed by the storm. He should have checked her tonight anyway, with all this thunder and lightning: it was quite disturbing to realise how much he had allowed his sweet enchanting Miriam to come between him and his responsibilities. Still, better late than never. He dragged an old pullover over his pyjamas and headed purposefully towards the stairs.

He had always insisted the dogs should sleep in the house – the best burglar alarm invented, as he'd often said to Miriam, and he made a point of speaking to them as he went to collect his boots. He was surprised, therefore, to find them all up, restless and grumbling, when he came back into the hall. Perhaps it was their obvious edginess that made him start violently as he caught sight of Justin, or maybe it was just the outlandish cut of the creature and the noiseless way he flitted round the end of the banisters.

"Sit, Bonnie!" he said loudly. "Off to your baskets! And that means you too Sheba . . . Jester . . ." Somehow it was easier to announce himself like this than to make a direct overture to Justin, though now that he had begun, the subject led him on quite naturally.

"Hope they didn't frighten you?" he said cheerfully. "Got Patsy Braithwaite down a few weekends ago . . . Well, you know Patsy! Had a few over the eight as usual and went to sleep in the conservatory. We were scattered all over the place, playing billiards, some of us in the gun room, and nobody missed him at bedtime; so come three o'clock, when poor old Patsy surfaced, he found everyone else had gone up."

He paused, pulling on his gumboot, suddenly wishing he had not embarked on the story; for Justin of course did not know Patsy Braithwaite, nor probably anyone remotely like him, and that totally ruined the humour of the tale. It was one of the summer's best anecdotes and all his friends, who'd known Patsy for years, found it irresistible: the picture of him swaying across the hall, his discomfiture when the dogs advanced snarling upon him, his precipitant flight, the way he had squeezed his huge frame out through the library window: and then how old Bertrand d'Arcy, awakened in his room above by the baying and the commotion, had looked down to see what appeared to be a fleeing intruder – and true to the same blood that had once poured boiling oil from a mediaeval turret, had emptied the contents of his chamber pot most accurately over his head . . .

A marvellous lark; it had made the weekend for everyone: and now he resented the way Justin's blank polite expression was making him feel foolish as he recounted it. Yet he supposed you should really feel sorry for the fellow, who was clearly quite out of his depth on these occasions, when Miriam insisted on bringing him down to Coombe. In fact, now he came to think of it, he wondered why she had invited him. Just look at the man, if indeed that was how one should describe him. Could he not afford to get himself a decent pair of pyjamas or a dressing gown? Not that he objected to nightshirts in principle – old Bertrand d'Arcy, for instance, always wore one, but this awful garment! He had never seen anything like it. It resembled a cotton vest, but immensely elongated, a tight tube that ended well below the knee; and it was not even plain or striped as nightshirts should be, it was printed all over with tiny teddy bears, exactly like some of the stuff that had arrived in Jamie's nursery, with the neck and armholes bound in shocking pink.

He looked away uncomfortably. He'd met pansies before goodness knows; there had even been some floating round at school, though he'd cleared off pretty fast when he found them in his vicinity, and he knew well enough it was best to treat them as ordinary human beings and attempt to conceal one's distaste.

"Well, I'm just going out," he declared, taking care to speak civilly if rather coldly. "I've got a mare in the stables who's getting near her time."

"Oh . . . really?" said Justin vaguely.

"Do you happen to have another torch you could lend me?" he added unexpectedly. "I was just going out myself. It's so stuffy inside tonight what with all this thunder and everything. I don't seem able to get to sleep."

Victor looked down at his hand, and the big heavy-duty torch that he held to light his journey. There were other torches no doubt, but he did not know where to find them. He could hardly go out himself, his way illuminated, and leave his guest to flounder around in the dark. He sighed; hospitality was hospitality, and no Templeton of any worth ever abused it.

"I don't think so," he said. "But come along with me if you want to. I expect Molly will be all right anyway. I shouldn't be very long."

There was a pause, a longer pause than he was expecting. His gaze fell to the floor where Justin's feet, encased incongruously in espadrilles, held his attention. Around one ankle was a curious torque with rough turquoise stones set in silver, very similar, almost identical to a bracelet he had sometimes seen Miriam wear. For some reason it riled him; it seemed much more objectionable than the extraordinary nightshirt, and he cursed the pointless good manners that had prompted his last remark. What did it matter if Justin lost his way? For all he cared he could fall and drown in the river, or break his leg, or get struck down by lightning. It only made it worse to see that the fellow himself lacked enthusiasm for the expedition and was only agreeing to it in a lack-lustre way. It did not help either to find that the front door had jammed quite solidly, as it sometimes did when a downpour swelled the timber, and that they had to tug at it together, in constrained co-operation, before they could make it open at all. As they stepped out into the pall of the night the single beam from the torch still held them fast, linked awkwardly but unavoidably to one another, without any acceptable excuse to break away.

Yet the night – the night was persuasive. It permeated, it overpowered the clouded atmosphere between them. It changed their uneasy alliance into something approaching companionship.

"The smell ..." said Justin wonderingly.

And he responded gruffly, himself overpowered by the sweetness of the aroma. "Yes, the smell ... It's like this sometimes, if you can catch it. It's so strong because the drought has ended. It's been brought out by the rain."

They walked slowly, absorbing the odour of fallen leaves, of latent growth; the thick potent scent of the earth renewed again. They stopped by unspoken consent beneath the big willow that stood at the bend of the river and watched the water rush violently past them, sucking and swirling round the base of the tree as though wishing to uproot it. Yesterday the stream had been clear and almost motionless, a harmless decorative trickle with just enough water left for the fat brown trout it sheltered, but tonight, in spate, it was muddy, fierce, unrecognisable. It surged triumphantly through the small arc of their torchlight, bruising its banks and bowing the reeds and grasses until they sank beneath it, bearing along with it leaves and twigs and branches that twisted and writhed in front of them as they swept in and out of the dark.

Justin did not speak and Victor strained his eyes against the blackness, anxious to find out whether the bank had broken on the further side. The land was lower there, and he'd spent quite a lot on drainage ... but the circle of light did not reach it, and he stared instead at the torrent of unruly water that hurried on so purposefully through the night. He had never found the current so fast, or the river so high before, and it did not please him to come upon it like this, swollen and dirty and rebellious. He hoped it would not do some tiresome and expensive damage, like flooding the mead cottages, or sweeping away the ford.

He shifted uneasily: all that would be a nuisance of course, but it did not explain his disquiet. He wished William or Hester or one of the boys was standing here beside him, or indeed any one of his legion of fishing friends. How he loved to fish! And how splendid was the company afforded by the fishing! He had always taken care to stock and tend the river so that the offer of a rod there should remain a coveted prize. Yes, any one of them would do: even Patsy, with his ready jokes and the hip flask in his pocket, or his father's crony, lame old Laurence Fairtlough, with his fifty years of uproarious angler's tales. Any one of them would do, would restore at once the sensible contentment that he usually felt when he stood beside his river, would prevent its turbulence vibrating through him in this unacceptable way.

He swung his torch round angrily upon Justin. He had always despised illogical sensitivity – a feeble and unseemly emotion for a man. It was bad enough to fall prey to it on occasions without finding that you were sharing your feelings with an uncongenial queer. He had no wish to understand his silence, or join in his abstraction. It was infuriating to see him stand, as though bemused by the power and movement, in an attitude that would have made any normal human being doubt the evidence of his eyes.

"Best get on!" he said curtly, and swung away without waiting for an answer. Let the fellow follow or stay behind as it pleased him. For his part he must see to it finally that Miriam ended this absurd association. She was young and she must be guided; he really could not be expected to tolerate such company.

The decision had a bracing effect; it made him feel much better. By the time he had crossed the pasture and was striding down the gravelled avenue to the stables, the light pad of Justin's footfalls beside him had ceased to aggravate him at all. He would certainly cause some embarrassment tomorrow, he had known all along that he should never have agreed to this godfather business, but that would be an end of it. He saw now that he had been much too lenient, indulging the most annoying of Miriam's attitudes and opinions when he should have taken a far stronger stand. 'A bloody saint' indeed! From now on he would see that she was steered, tenderly but firmly, towards a more orthodox frame of mind.

He would start by persuading her to take a more positive interest in the horses. Good horsemanship, after all, was his one real talent, the field in which he held undisputed sway. Judgement and knowledge and nerve, he had all those; and something else, a kind of instinct, a communication that extended his ability a long way beyond the boundaries of experience or skill. No matter that it was a faintly suspect quality, a little too odd and intense to be one that you were wholly proud of – he knew that it was secretly recognised and coveted everywhere. He would try to explain all this to Miriam when he brought her down to the stables with him in the mornings. It was just the right moment too, since Brookman had at last gone off on holiday, having satisfied himself that all the bloodstock were safely foaled. It was hard to make Miriam see that Brookman's curt manners were not designed to upset her; or indeed that his good opinion was a tribute not easily won . . .

He quickened his pace, remembering his head groom's endless vigilance, and how readily he had assured him he would keep an eye on Molly until she dropped her foal. "Just a glance before I turn in. I know you're afraid of the lads forgetting to check her." And he chuckled goodhumouredly, thinking fussy, loyal old bastard, anything to keep him happy. "You don't leave much to trust these days, do you?" he had added affectionately . . . But now, it appeared, he could no longer be trusted himself. He passed hurriedly in front of the Brookmans' house, where it stood empty and reproachful beside the stable gateway, and reaching the old pony's loosebox snapped on the electric light.

8

The mare stood facing him, and for a moment, half-blinded by the brightness, he thought that nothing was amiss with her. Then he saw that the bed was trampled, and wet where the waters must have broken, and that a straggle of mucus was trailing down her flank. As he pushed back the door and she wheeled round towards the manger, he felt a dull lurch of panic of which he was ashamed. She was in the last stages of labour, her hind legs painfully straddled, and instead of the two legs that should have protruded from her vulva there was only a single hoof.

He stared at the foot with horror. How he hated the thought of a wrongly presented foetus. Birth was strange enough, risky enough, messy enough for him, without any abnormalities or complications: but as he spoke to the pony – "Steady up there, Molly! Easy now, old lady!" the good words worked their magic upon his stomach and the foolish moment of terror was instantly over and done. He began to whistle tunelessly through his teeth, studying the mare with professional concentration.

A leg back was not too bad: he knew that so long as it was speedily corrected the foal stood a reasonable chance of being born alive. But speed was of the essence: a long delay and the umbilical cord would eventually rupture; or the foetus would simply attempt to breathe, its lungs stimulated by the prolonged contractions, and fill its lungs with the uterine fluids that it inhaled. It was all a question of time, and this mare had been foaling for far too long to please him, he could tell it by the weary dispirited manner in which she stood. Her damp flanks were no longer heaving with regular muscular spasm but rose and fell dejectedly in time to a shallow breathing that spoke all too plainly of exhaustion and distress.

He took the one leg in his hand, knowing it would be dry before he touched it, the short hair crisp as a bristle underneath his finger tips. Yes, a lot too long. On a night like this, how could he have failed to check her? It was rotten bad stockmanship, no other name would do. He had sometimes wondered lately if perhaps he *was* slipping, becoming too casual and inattentive. But had his marriage – had Miriam really reduced him to this?

He hurled the thought aside. The thing was done, and this was no time for self-examination. Just now the only question to be settled was whether he called out the vet. If he did, an hour or more would certainly be wasted, and that sort of delay would mean losing all hope for the foal: better, then, to attempt the job himself, and with a bit of luck he still might save it. It was pure coincidence if the decision rescued him from humiliation; that if he involved the vet, the whole countryside would learn of his irresponsible behaviour, of how he had left a mare to foal for eight hours, unattended, in the worst thunderstorm of the year . . .

He pushed Justin aside and strode across to the tack room, wrenching open the first aid cupboard and flicking on the lights in the yard. "Find some buckets!" he shouted rudely over his shoulder. "Find some buckets and fill them with water. And look sharp about it, will you? We haven't got much time left." It relieved him to speak to Justin like that, he couldn't think why he had ever struggled to treat him as an equal: God knows he'd have thrown him out quick enough if he had applied as a stable hand. Still, perhaps he was better than nothing, and he hoped the experience would shock him. Bloody fairy . . . He took down the ropes that hung with their knotted loops at the ready, and helped himself to soap and a towel and some lubricating fluid, and a box of suppositories to prevent infection in the mare.

He had stripped to the waist and was sanding the floor by the time Justin came with the water. He took the buckets brusquely, without thanking him, and pushed Molly's halter roughly into his hands.

"Hold her head," he said. "And for Christ's sake don't upset her. If I tie her she might throttle when she feels like going down."

Justin took the rope apprehensively and he looked at him with loathing. He wished suddenly that Molly was one of his thoroughbreds, who would rear and fight and panic and be quieted by no one but himself. But of course that was senseless, things were quite bad enough with a quiet and experienced pony . . . He plunged his arm into the bucket and lathered it up to the shoulder, and then began to insert it, slowly and resolutely, into the dark fleshy recesses of the birth canal.

Immediately he was absorbed, swallowed up in the blind world that engulfed his fingers. He had no time now for thoughts that were better left unformulated, nor any need for sight or hearing either; all his concentration was centred on his sense of touch. He could feel the nose already, and the whole head coming through the cervix, and as far as he could tell the foal was still alive. He began to push it backwards, forcing himself to wait for the pauses between the muscular contractions, and he turned his body sideways as his arm went deeper, so that his cheek pressed tightly against the sodden hide. There! The head was back at last, and his own hand with it, groping among the warm wet membranes that lay in the uterus itself. Legs . . . There seemed to be a mass of legs. But here at last was the knee that he was seeking. He ran his hand down to the fetlock, pulling it up and easing it gradually forward through the cervix, with the sharp hoof cupped protectively in his hand. As he drew it triumphantly out through the vaginal passage, he could feel that the mare, as if in answer to his unspoken wishes, was beginning to sink to her knees.

"Get back here and pull!" In a fury of haste he looped the ropes over the fetlocks and gestured Justin down beside him on the stable floor.

The last critical moment before an assisted birth was always full of tension, but tonight he felt literally sick with the worry and suspense of it, as if his whole judgement and reputation was resting upon this foal. What was more, he could see that poor Molly was spent, and was now so dejected she'd offer him little assistance; he would have to provide all the strength that she was lacking, and the terror of physical failure was staring him in the face. Would he be fit enough, man enough, to produce both the power and the stamina that were needed? As he picked up the ropes he could feel the adrenalin pumping through his body as though he was under starter's orders for some hazardous steeple chase.

He was scarcely aware of Justin as they sweated and strained together, though they lay wedged shoulder to shoulder, with their arms overlapping on the ropes. There was no message now from his brain save the one he directed towards his protesting muscles, nor any thought strong enough to challenge his determination to endure. And then, abruptly, the whole thing was over. The head had appeared, dangling limply outside the vulva, and with one last heave the rest of the body followed, slithering forward in a cascade of fluid and landing heavily across their knees.

He leapt to his feet and bestrode the bedraggled body, bending over it in an agony of anticipation and propping its head against his leg. It was whole and unblemished, so new and so lovely that he trembled, and the sight of Molly's white star, emblazoned on its forehead, caused his throat to constrict in a very unmasculine way. But it still wasn't breathing. Not yet. It *would* breathe. It *must* breathe . . . He would make it! He had frequently revived an exhausted foal.

He seized a piece of straw and pushed it up one of the nostrils, moving it vigorously to and fro. It would shake its head in a minute, and then with a gasp it would suddenly be breathing. He had seen it happen so often. Why wasn't it happening now?

He dropped the straw. He could feel the heart, still faintly beating; and its eyes, though vacant and unresponsive, remained as clear as glass. It was going to live. Just one breath and it would be living. He straightened the forelegs and scooped up the straw to support the flaccid body so that it rested erect upon its breast. What did Brookman say? 'Just go on. Never stop. Always give it a good ten minutes . . .' All right then: that was what he would do.

He made his mind consciously blank as he settled himself astride it with the small bony diaphragm motionless under his hands. Depress and release. Depress and release. Let the rhythm absorb you, drug you, take you over. In and out. Up and down. Smooth and regular. Counting, counting, counting . . . In and out. Press and rest. (Keep your mind empty, you'll know soon enough if its breathing.) Calm and blank. Press and rest. (How long is there left? Mustn't think, mustn't pause to wonder.) Never stop. Just go on. One, two, three . . .

"Victor! VICTOR!"

He heard him, of course. And he knew what he wanted to tell him. Up and down. Press and rest. His movements slowed ponderously, unwillingly. 'Just go on.' But the pendulum was stopping. He must face the fact there was no hope any more. In a moment he'd come to terms with it. Get the whole thing back in proportion. Just one foal, foolishly lost. It could happen to anyone – why was he shaking with anger? Why this frightening, almost murderous bitterness?

His palms slipped reluctantly over the curve of the rib cage and came to rest on the saturated straw. He hung there, his shoulders sagging, suddenly weary beyond all measure, crouched like an animal on hands and knees. The blankness that he had courted still offered him a refuge, and he let his head fall forward with his chin resting on his breast. For a moment he was blind to the body beneath him and to the brightly lighted stable. He saw Miriam, only Miriam, as he saw her sometimes on the very edge of sleep. Miriam laughing, Miriam loving, Miriam sweeping all things before her – custom and convention, duty and friendship and obligation, all carried along on the same enchanted tide. But her features were hardening, he could see them changing. Here was Miriam bored and sulky; scornful, impatient, discontented; Miriam stranger still, grown unpredictable and furtive, gone clandestinely from a gathering, out of a room . . . Seeking what? Some excitement, some prize that he never could give her? Some experience he was not equipped to share?

He lifted his head, and there before him was the life that he had squandered; Molly's foal, Jamie's foal, grimly accusatory in death. He had held its existence in his hands, and by default he had witlessly destroyed it. The efficiency and speed that he had brought to the delivery only made his earlier fecklessness more impossible to excuse. He was not some incompetent egghead, some precious city dilletante, but a breeder of great experience who was losing his grip on the job. And this foal, starkly dead – it was only the tip of the iceberg, a stern warning, an object lesson. And my God, it had opened his eyes!

It had opened his eyes: he would see that it opened Miriam's. There would be no more play-acting, no more airy fairy ways. She was his wife, his companion, she was going to share this disaster, and he did not care if the sight would cause her pain. In fact he welcomed it; he positively desired it. He wanted her to understand what lay at the root of this horrible wastage; to see her stare at it, pale and shocked and sickened, her attention brought back from wherever it was it had strayed.

He stumbled to his feet, half dazed, unprepared for the numbness in his muscles. "Don't touch anything," he said harshly. "Leave it just as it is, do you hear?" He paused. "She's not getting some prettied up version she'll forget in a day or two."

He began to pull on his pyjama jacket, aware for the first time that he was shaking, that the cold sweat was trickling in rivulets down his chest.

"What the hell are you talking about?" said Justin.

The words were mildly spoken, as if they were designed to soothe him, and as his head emerged from the neck of his jersey he saw that the man was conspicuously absorbed in watching poor Molly, who was up and nosing anxiously at the body of her foal. Yes, Justin was sorry for him, giving him time to pull himself together. Pity, coming from that quarter, seemed too great an insult to bear.

"I'm fetching Miriam!" He had not meant to raise his voice, but he found that he was shouting. "She's going to see what's happened in this stable. And it's bloody well staying the way that it is right now!"

He had felt it so keenly, the absolute need for her presence; yet as soon as he spoke them, the words made the impulse unreal. It was impossible to imagine Miriam here, in this stench of birth and sweat and urine. His eyes flickered over the shambles: the discarded ropes, the spilt soap flakes, the upturned buckets, the blood and afterbirth, dung and mucus – he had seen it all a score of times before. He could not recall what it was that he had glimpsed here, so important that it had to be kept intact for Miriam, nor what had induced him to rave about going to fetch her; it had surely been more than the sight of this dismal stable with a dead foal on the floor? He hesitated, trying to fathom his own confusion, but before he could speak again Justin had gripped him by the shoulder and pinioned him with his back against the door.

"Cool it down," he said. He spoke evenly, almost politely, but his hold was so painful, his action so unexpected, that for a second Victor simply gaped at him as if he had been stunned. His face was very close. It was like something hewn in granite; far stronger, far craggier than he remembered. Perhaps it was the shadow cast by the unshaded light bulb, but he had the uncomfortable feeling that he had never really looked at it before.

"Cool it down," he was repeating. "And leave Miriam out of this carnage. It's important to you, I know that – but it isn't her scene at all. It will give her nightmares I grant you, but they'll just turn her off completely. As you'd see for yourself if you'd any wits left in your head."

He glared at him, incredulous. This misfit, this ballet dancer, this fey and pathetic pervert, was reading him a lesson on how to look after his wife. It was totally insufferable. It burst through all constraints that good manners imposed upon him.

"You clear off!" he cried wildly. "What the hell do you know about how to deal with women? Just go back to your boys and your dancing and leave Miriam to me."

He spat out the last words with venom, and felt Justin let go of him, startled. And instantly he was appallingly ashamed. To have dragged this filth into the open! How embarrassing. How uncivilised. And what the devil could he do about it now? He longed to turn away, to dissolve this degrading conflict as if it had never happened, but his eyes were transfixed by the curious expression that was growing on Justin's face.

"So that's it," he said at last. "That explains it. I've often wondered . . ." His eyes met Victor's, bright with mockery and comprehension. "You poor bloody fool, you've convinced yourself that I'm gay."

He sat down abstractedly, perched on the rail of the manger. "Or did she tell you?" he continued. "Why, Jesus Christ! I can see that she did, the little vixen . . ."

His voice petered out, and he paused then, but just for a minute.

"Well, cheer up!" he went on. "Don't look so glum about it, Victor! Aren't you pretty relieved that my vices are so straightforward?"

And he suddenly flung his head back on the hay in the manger and laughed aloud.

9

As a finishing touch, though it hardly needed one with the embroidered tray cloth and the last of the Royal Doulton, Dorothy put a small spray of pink chrysanthemums on Father's breakfast tray. She smiled down at it serenely. It would give him pleasure to use the beautiful china, and if he broke the cup or ruined the tray cloth, well then so much the better. It would add to her punishment when crockery and linen became of significance to her again. There was no knowing when that might happen, when the moment would arrive at which her thoughts and her feelings united: but since even this uncertainty had not begun to matter, she knew there were still a number of hours in hand.

She no longer felt worried or frightened during these peculiar respites, indeed she had come to expect them, even to enjoy them in a way. She had found that no effort of will could bring on the remorse that would eventually overcome her, for the cogs between will and emotion were in temporary disarray. It was always the same: her mind clear and sharp, aware of the shame and the broken resolutions, recording with complete detachment the diminished stock of tranquillisers, the empty bottle of wine; recording too the disorder round her desk where the scrawled sheets of paper were littered all over the carpet, signs of the vice that lured her with its offer of catharsis, and yet led inevitably towards disgrace.

She also perceived, with the same aloof composure, just how deeply she soon would suffer for what she had done. How she'd shrink from herself when she read what was spewed on the paper, the wild unnatural outpourings of a person disowned and shunned. She would feel sick then, she might even *be* sick to complete her degradation, for this doppel-ganger who denounced her was not merely insalubrious; she was sinister and powerful and viciously destructive, she made ordinary Dorothy quake with fear. But this morning 'fear' was only a word, like penitence, or insanity, or revulsion. She knew what they meant, but their meaning could not touch her. Not yet. How merciful that 'yet', by the same miraculous process, had been rendered harmless as well!

The room was filling with steam. She glided through it and switched off the forgotten kettle, pouring what was left of the water onto the leaves in the pot. It was not the usual tea pot, but the silver one they kept for best occasions. She had taken it out of the cupboard as a matter of course this morning, knowing it would complete the perfection of Father's breakfast tray.

"Here we are then!" Father's window faced east, and the morning sun made her stagger backwards for a moment, but she managed to reach the invalid table without spilling anything, and to lower the tray safely to rest. As she swung it across his knees with a little flourish of self-satisfaction she saw he was eyeing her warily, with the speculative regard of a captive, halfway between cunning and servility. It was plain to her what he was thinking: that her smiling face must be tested before it could be trusted, like a rotten branch that might fail to bear your weight.

Well, she did not blame him. From the elevated state she inhabited this morning she could view her usual behaviour without flinching; could concede that this hour was normally the nadir of her day. Looking at it objectively, she reflected that she had often treated Father badly, that her haste and her unhappiness made her both rough and unkind. Not that she ever neglected him: she always left him washed and fed and tidy, but the dismal duties had increased and become more difficult to cope with calmly as the months dragged by. She had started to shave him long ago, and lately had begun to wash and feed him, overlooking his protestations with a furious impatience that was sharpened by despair. There was simply no time to indulge him. It was hard enough already not to scream as you waited for him to use his bedpan, when you knew that the traffic was growing more impossible with every second you delayed. Just occasionally, when the night had been bad and she had been dragged from sleep that had come too late to restore her, she had actually shouted at Father, berating him for his clumsiness and his stupidity, pointing out that she had her living to earn, and to earn it she must hurry. But she knew Father was not stupid. And today, immune from the guilt that would have made such an admission impossible, she could see that he positively feared her. His anxious eyes, myopic and bewildered without his glasses, still nervously searched her face.

She bent over and pecked his cheek. "There's no hurry," she said. "It's Saturday. And we're going to Jamie's christening, now do you remember? I've cooked you a lovely breakfast and you can eat it on your own."

His gaze dropped unwillingly as she gestured towards the table. He was clearly reluctant to miss any sign of sudden intolerance or irritation, as if he felt that properly forewarned, its impact might hurt him less.

Sometime, and quite soon, she knew the memory of his look would rend her. That it was empty of all censure, or of any desire to accuse her would not cause her to reproach herself the less: once and for always it condemned her as a bully, a piercing indictment which no amount of self-recrimination would hope to wipe away. Without doubt, she would suffer agonies of compunction.

As she fetched Father's glasses from the dressing table she put the reflection consciously on record, as though popping it into a filing cabinet for future reference. It could well be digested with some of last night's excesses, in conjunction, perhaps, with those hysterical never-to-be-posted letters to Auntie Maud. Letters wildly accepting her offer, saying take him, please come and take him. Do it quickly. Don't argue with us. Do not let us refuse you again. Saying, yes, he'd be happier with you. Can't you see that we both of us know it? Can't you hear that our protests are hollow? That we crave a pretext to agree? Can you not stretch the truth just a little: just this once, in the name of compassion? Stress your loneliness, call it a visit, any small subterfuge will suffice. 'A nice change of air for Alfred' – any flimsy excuse we could use to disguise the betrayal. Oh, Auntie, look at us! Perceive how we need our illusions. You could save them by bending, by simply pretending a little. But to prompt you would make it all pointless. It has got to come from you.

And it won't, she thought collectedly. Good, practical Aunt Maud, dutiful and upright. Uncompromisingly honest, looking facts in the face. You will not disguise your motives nor let us overlook that we now are annihilating each other. You will ask us plainly to declare it; to admit that you are rescuing me from intolerable strain, Father from unendurable dependency.

She smiled, picking up the spotless linen napkin, and gently wiped the egg yolk from his chin. Of course they would not do it. They would not reject, they would never renounce one another. She would still claim that her only true wish was to nurse him, that the virtual ruin of her career was a cross much more welcomed than shouldered, rendered weightless by daughterly love. And Father, poor Father, who suffered so much when she suffered, what more could he do than beg her unselfishly to leave him? He would never proclaim that her sacrifice was worthless, that her martyred frustration both terrified and distressed him, that he longed to be free of the burden of her care.

No, they could not do it. They must at all costs profess to want each other. To do otherwise would repudiate all the love and the tenderness that they had ever shared. And Aunt Maud was too honest to see that, far too forthright to come to their rescue. Her bald assessments would only shock and offend them, drawing them stubbornly together until their own loyalty destroyed them both. It's inevitable, she thought. There is no other possible outcome. The letter to Gaston Abbey can go into the fire with the rest.

"I'll just pour your tea." She leant across the tray and positioned the cup carefully, its handle angled towards his maimed right hand. Today, as always, she knew that he would obdurately attempt to use it, instead of employing his left hand, as she constantly urged him to do. But this morning such determination was merely touching, and she looked fondly down upon him as the cup left the saucer with a long juddering clatter and began to waver unsteadily into the air.

It was good to have time, for once, to admire his perseverance, and to enjoy again his distinctively beaky profile, both in their way so impressive to contemplate. And how fortunate that she was standing on his left side! From this angle the ravages of his stroke were practically invisible. The corner of his mouth was firm, his bushy eyebrow arched imposingly above his glasses, and his nose, so like her own though she carried it with none of his assurance, jutted out, fierce and commanding, as it had done in his prime.

She half-closed her eyes, cradling the tea pot in its knitted cosy. She could picture him plainly in such a variety of vestments, from the austere black cassock and billowing snowy surplice that had first enchanted her childhood, to the purple silk of the vest with the great cross hung upon it, the nobility of the mitre, the opulence of the embroidered cope. Dear Father, in tune with his God, who managed to carry such trappings with dignity, and yet remain humble. Who was only disappointed that his prayers for her own happiness remained unanswered, that his hopes of Victor . . . But that was of no importance. Victor was still there, was still her lifeline. She had written such nonsense to Victor last night, she remembered. Perhaps, as a treat to herself in honour of the christening, she could burn those demented pages unread?

Something plucked at her sleeve and she started, but it was only Father's fingers. He was speaking, she realised; had probably been speaking for some time too, to judge by the expression on his face. Well, his speech was often slurred and she frequently had to ask him to repeat things.

She took off her spectacles unhurriedly and began to clean the lenses with a tissue. "Could you just tell me that all over again?" she said.

"It's the bell," he was saying. "The door bell! Can't you hear it?" He shook her arm gently, as though she was asleep. "There it goes again! Aren't you going to answer it, darling? I expect that Nurse Rose has forgotten to bring her key."

"I'm going in a minute." She smiled amiably to reassure him. No point in telling him that a key would be of no use to Nurse Rose this morning, since last night she herself had both bolted and barred the door. It was strange now to think of the frenzy in which she had done so; how she'd slammed her side painfully against it as she tried to align the old bolts with their sockets, how she'd panted with haste as she swung up the heavy iron bar. It had seemed absolutely imperative to make the house impregnable to Humphrey, as if by asserting her power to shut him out completely she could prove that there still was a chance that he would change his mind. It had nearly worked too; there had been a moment, as she barricaded herself wildly against all invasion, when she had entirely forgotten that nobody would be hammering on the woodwork, that there never had been an assault upon her door. A pity that the anodyne had not lasted her through the evening. It would have fortified her, enabled her to withstand the onslaught of the doppel-ganger: she would have been spared from the terrible reaction that soon and inevitably must come her way.

Even now, as she dropped the cold iron bar, she distinctly experienced a foretaste of it, a trace of unease, a passing flicker of worry as to how far her sunny composure was going to deceive Nurse Rose. She must clear up the study, dispose of the bottles, the paper . . . But when the door burst open it was hard to take such matters seriously any more. How piercing, how thrilling, was the impact of this rainwashed morning! How incisively sharp the thin, pellucid air! And the colours! The lawn flamed golden with the fallen leaves of the chestnut, and the Michaelmas daisies, that yesterday had seemed faded and dusty, blazed hectically mauve and purple along the herbaceous border – so electrically mauve in fact, so overpoweringly purple, that they made her blink her eyes. Even the light was different; it was stronger, both clearer and harsher, as though the balance between sun and shadow had mysteriously changed.

Puzzled, she shifted her gaze towards the skyline, to where the trees, in their late summer grandeur, should be breaking the glare of the sun. But the heavy foliage was gone; she encountered instead the skeletal tracery of winter, a vivid unheralded winter with its stark branches etched theatrically against the sky. It was exquisite of course; but it was startling to find so abrupt, so savage a transformation. For an instant her heart jumped as if she had been ambushed, and when she attempted to return Nurse Rose's greeting she found that her fingers were clamped against her mouth rigidly, as though she were stifling a cry.

"What's the matter then, dear?"

How impatient and inquisitive they all seemed to be this morning! She was sure she had heard Father make the same intrusive remark. It was just as well that she was feeling so benevolent and abstracted, or she might have been driven to some unkind retort.

As it was, she stepped back as if she had not heard the question, and with a politeness that veered towards the gracious, ushered Nurse Rose before her into the hall.

"Such a morning!" she exclaimed. "Such a wonderful day for the Christening!"

After all, why should she trouble to offer Nurse Rose any explanation? The front door was her own, to secure or leave open as she pleased.

"I've a few things to see to," she continued in an airy manner. "So perhaps you could start to get the Bishop dressed. I've laid all his things out for you, but it's bound to take longer than usual."

She turned away dismissively, but looked back as she reached the study observing Nurse Rose with a little tremor of excitement as she disappeared behind Father's door. It was such a long time since she had seen him dressed up for an outing, though they took him for drives sometimes, wrapped up in his overcoat in the back of the car. Yet today, despite his handicaps, she knew he would still look distinguished and arresting, rejuvenated by his dark suit, his best shoes, his stiff and simple collar and, serving to underline the dignified restraint of the rest of his appearance, the dashing magenta of his bishop's vest.

It was then, even as she smiled, that the first black miasma engulfed her, erupting from its hiding place like a genie released from a bottle, extinguishing her happiness, obliterating her contentment as effortlessly as a cloud obscures the sun. Seven ages of man: from the newborn child in the shawl to Father, dressed and displayed in his wheelchair like a waxwork, his speech incoherent, his concentration failing, his poor lopsided mouth as prone as any baby's to dribble and drool. Father stripped of all dignity, helpless. At the full turn of the wheel, nothing more than a ghastly travesty of the infant at the font.

She clung to the door jamb, trembling. It would pass. It would pass quite quickly. It always did pass, this first searing and ferocious arousal of pain. It just meant she'd touched on a raw spot, where emotion, like some hidden volcano, lay particularly close to the surface; but the sanctuary, though crumbling, could be saved to protect her still. She must simply nurture it carefully, tread warily to avoid the weak spots. If nothing untoward undermined it she might keep it from complete disintegration until the day was done.

She gave herself a few moments, and then crossed to the welter of papers, shoving them into the bureau with averted face. She would not examine them now, would not contemplate the unspeakable things she would find that she had written. Just a page or two would be certain to reactivate the genie, and a second time he would not be so easily dismissed. She turned the key in her desk; it would all have been easier if she could have used the dustbin, but Nurse Rose had revealed a disconcerting tendency to poke and pry. Deftly, she inserted the empty bottles behind Collected Sermons, wiped the glass on the sleeve of her cardigan and replaced it on the tray. Yes, already she felt a lot better; she had almost regained the sublime state of vacancy that had been so rudely and unexpectedly invaded. She was pleased to feel mild surprise only, quite unclouded by shame or panic, when she noticed how many sedatives were missing from the box. What a pity they had started to put them into packets. It was all too easy to press out those little tinfoil bubbles without noticing how quickly you were getting through the cards. Now with bottles, at least you could see exactly what you were doing, though the argument seemed to fall down when it came to the wine.

With a frown she gathered up the discarded squares of plastic, and striking a match, watched intently as they liquefied and shrivelled, vanishing among the ashes of the empty grate.

They managed Father quite comfortably: Nurse Rose's car was not large, but it was specially adapted, and they always used it these days if he had to be moved about. The height was just right, you could slide him across without feeling that you might drop him on the roadside, and with the rear seats down, the wheelchair fitted satisfactorily into the back. The only drawback was that this left no room for a second passenger, so that when the chair was needed, Dorothy was forced to take her own car as well. Usually this was a nuisance, both more tiring and more expensive, but today she was pleased to secure a few moments to herself. There would be plenty of people to help Nurse Rose off with Father, and she had even sent them on a little early so that he might have time to rest before the ceremony and recover from the hassle of the drive.

In her bedroom she started her own preparations without anxiety. This was pleasing in itself, for her rule about forward planning did not always pay such a handsome dividend. She had decided weeks ago upon two alternative outfits, and now that the heatwave was evidently over, the grey homemade cotton could be put aside. That left only the jersey wool dress, confronting her with its matching jacket on the back of the wardrobe door. It was plainly a suitable garment; she could not understand why she felt such a lack of enthusiasm for it. Perhaps it was because it reminded her so vividly of her old friend Angela Beale? Though that would be shockingly ungrateful. It was providential that Angela passed on her clothes with such generosity; they were invariably a great deal more expensive than anything she could afford. It was probably having to alter them that made them look rather shapeless, and of course their ideas about colour had never been quite the same.

She took down the hanger and carried it across to her mirror, holding it against her face in the unequivocal morning light. But naturally it had not changed: it was not, and it never had been, a material that became her. Still, at least it was safe, there was no danger of feeling conspicuous in it, there was something particularly self-effacing about that amorphous shade of pinkish beige. And what luck that it went with her hat, with the faintly rose tinted silk turban. She resented money spent on hats, now that nobody else ever wore them. But Father was very old fashioned about such matters, and what use in setting out to praise the Almighty bareheaded, when He knew you were flagrantly offending your near and dear?

She began to reach up for the hat when she caught sight of Miriam's clothing. She had swathed it neatly in a plastic bag from the cleaners, but even through the wrapping it seemed more distinctive than anything else on the rail. 'Why Dorothy, you look . . . different!' She took the bag out; she must not forget to bring it with her. Odd, how well the clothes had fitted, when this dress she was wearing of Angie's still sagged in all sorts of unexpected places although she had tried industriously to take it in. She turned back for the turban, and as she raised her arms she was suddenly swept by a most disconcerting sensation, as if the long skirt was still swirling about her ankles, as if she still stood on the ladder, aglow and on tiptoe, the flowers in her hands. Reaching up. Reaching up in a silk shirt that shone like a garnet, and that broke all the rules she was following now with such care: never bow to an impulse, or swerve from a well planned decision: avoid anything that may attract attention, the eye-catching, the gaudy, the bizarre.

It was then that she chose the scarlet hat, or rather that it came to be in her fingers, upon her head. Rapidly, daringly she spun round to the looking glass. It was certainly a sensation; and after all, she had broken the rules already, long ago, when she bought it in that brittle ethereal summer before Victor became engaged. She had purchased all sorts of strange things then, flouting the guidelines with a sudden and frenzied abandon. It must have been something to do with her breakdown coming on.

Yet just look at this hat! There was no doubt that it did something for her. Indeed it was so gaudy, so ebullient, with its enormous brim and all those drooping feathers that it suddenly brought out of limbo the image of Miriam's mother Grace. She tried not to think of Grace these days: it was frightening to reflect on what had happened since her marriage, but on this quiescent morning the memory was isolated, like one solitary frame of a film, and it brought her no distress. In fact, it produced quite a glow, for Grace, in the years of her flowering, had been more than usually lovely; she had been incandescent, voluptuous, she had a knack of attracting attention which everybody, whether or not they disapproved of her, had been unable to ignore. And how they *had* disapproved; even then, when she had not really understood the reason, she had known that 'poor Marcus and Eleanor' were pitiable because of Grace; and Hester and Lizzie, her own age but much more knowing, had giggled about her in corners, nudging each other rudely as she passed. There had been an appalling to-do when Grace had finally (and tardily, for Templeton girls were expected to marry early) announced her unsuitable match. The family had closed ranks in the end, but the loss of face throughout the county had been humiliating. Lady Alice had visited dressmakers with a tight-lipped air of tolerance, and you knew that Hester and Lizzie were rendered up as bridesmaids not with pleasure but resignation, as a sort of sacrifice in support of Poor Marcus and Poor Eleanor, who had had the misfortune to spawn such a changeling of a child.

Looking back now, Dorothy was almost glad that she had

been so foolishly innocent: at least she had been able to savour, without prurience or criticism, the gift of Grace's exceptional loveliness. She had watched her face from the choir stalls as she stood by the side of her disquietingly flashy bridegroom, and her eyes had strayed over the bridesmaids, six or eight of them behind her: bright pretty girls in pastel dresses, with flowers in their hair, selfconsciously eligible, infinitely ordinary. 'You meaner beauties of the night' – her head had always been ringing with poetry in those days, and during Grace's wedding she remembered how stubbornly her mind had become obsessed with the rhythm of Wotton's tribute to Elizabeth of Bohemia: how she had whispered it inaudibly when really she should have been praying; and how, looking over a congregation smug with so many delicate violets, she had longed to have the courage to leap to her feet and declaim it – 'What are you when the rose is blown?'

Poor Grace. Poor lost exquisite Grace. She must not think of her now or the genie might break through, the sweet transient peace be shattered. Rather she must dwell positively on the good that had come of the union, on Miriam for instance, who had made dearest Victor so astonishingly happy . . . though unfortunately her slightly vulgar prettiness seemed to come from Dickie rather than from her mother, and could hardly be said to hold anything of the rose. Well, she would think of Jamie then, not just as Victor's son, but also, incredible as it seemed, as Grace's grandchild. How confusing these slips of generation tended to be! And she would wear this hat for Grace as well, not just for Grace the radiant girl, but for Grace the ravaged junkie, those two irreconcilable figures that the Good Lord, whose ways in so many respects bewildered her, had designed as one entity.

10

At the bottom of the lane, where it joined the village street of Coombe Bassett, a sign to the Manor Stud directed you to the left. Going that way you presently arrived at the main road, and found the demesne wall facing you, with the entrance to the stable avenue already in view along it a few hundred yards away to the right. But the wall ran on for two miles before it reached the front gates, and Dorothy always assured herself that it was shorter, as well as a great deal more pleasant, to approach the house by Abbot's Corner. In fact, although shorter in distance, the private road took you much longer, for it snaked circuitously downwards towards the river and then pursued it closely round its many narrow bends. Even the uphill straight that followed Abbot's Bridge was checked by the main road that lay across the gateway, although occasionally Dorothy had been horrified to find herself on the other side of it with no recollection of stopping at all. But no doubt she had done so: it was just that the gates were so dominant and overwhelming that the sight of them made you forget such incidental details. Standing open beneath the curved flanking walls and the stately arch that framed them, they drew you hypnotically forward, as though into a familiar and perpetually enticing embrace.

It was really this view of the gates, the sensation of seeing them above you, of rising up to meet them, that made the navigation of the shortcut an insignificant price to pay. As she rounded the last bend she was always touched with a quiver of excitement, as if she was about to see a work of art unveiled. It never grew stale either, for although the subject remained constant, the treatment was always, and sometimes breathtakingly, varied. In the evenings for instance, especially in summer when the sinking sun shone full upon it, the stone would glow and blush in welcome, absorbing and reflecting the carmine light from the west; and if you were lucky a window pane in one of the lodges would catch up a ray and fling it back down the valley, flashing gold and scarlet as though it was aflame. The mornings were wonderful too, although with the light behind them the gates seemed loftier and less approachable, and even when the sun began to slant round and shine obliquely upon them, the shadows they cast were sharp and black and cold. But she'd learnt not to let that hurt her: to other people the entrance might look forbidding, but surely she had earned a warm and friendly greeting? Since childhood she had used and loved these gates, had hurried through them more eagerly than if they had led to her own home.

At the foot of the lane then, she always turned away from the main road: right and immediately left again, a process that needed no thought. Why should she be sitting with her hand poised uncertainly over the indicator, peering up and down the village street as if she had never seen it before? It was true that yesterday she had been particularly upset by meeting Miriam and Justin, but then in many ways it had been an unfortunate moment, what with the cloudburst and the puncture and the terrifying way they had skidded towards her car. Yet it had not been unexpected: for a long time now she had feared that she might meet Miriam, had felt increasingly resentful that she should be using the lane at all. It had not been so bad to start with; then she had simply been astonished, had assumed her appearance was due to some sort of mistake. Everyone knew that Miriam liked speeding. It was not until she had mentioned the matter to Victor, pointing out that the main road would bring his wife home much more quickly, that she had appreciated how the thrill of speed and risk were intertwined. It was more fun, Victor explained, for Miriam to drive too fast down to Abbot's Corner than to eat up the miles on the main road — just because it *was* dangerous, chancy, altogether a more skilful and challenging game. At least there were no other cars there; it could be her own private race track. But he had sighed as he spoke, and the look on his face, bewildered and helpless and worried, had caused her a pang of pity that made her feel quite ill, and left her sick with indignation at Miriam's thoughtlessness. It had also strengthened her resolve not to be driven away from her own time-honoured pathways, and above all not to be robbed of that lifegiving, that constant yet ever-changing first sight of the gates of Coombe. She would not be deflected by Miriam, and if this extraordinary reluctance to follow her usual routine was simply caused by yesterday's encounter, then she certainly must resist it; to do anything else would be shamefully weak willed.

She shifted her hand to the gearstick, moving it ponderously as if a heavy weight was dragging down her fingers. Right and immediately left: she must find some train of thought that would banish her trepidation and make it easier for her to turn the steering wheel. She frowned in concentration: 'when I was a child . . .' When she was a child she used to cycle over to Coombe Manor in the holidays, though for lessons she would wait for their governess at the corner of the main road, forsaking aesthetic pleasures for the comfort of Miss Beasley's car; and also of Miss Beasley's company, so stimulating and reassuring, so essential to her status in the schoolroom at Coombe.

Her fingers relaxed. Miss Beasley had died long ago but the memory of her affection and encouragement was still consoling. From the very beginning, long before the boys were removed and sent away to prep school, she had been her governess's favourite, and their relationship had only been enhanced by the fact that the Templeton girls could be curiously obtuse and insensitive, although they were perfectly intelligent in their way. Now, with her own experience behind her, she reflected that it must have been all too easy for Miss Beasley to typecast Hester and Lizzie. She herself had met so many girls exactly like them, girls with good brains on whom education was manifestly wasted; who could learn, but would grow no richer for their learning; impossible to awaken, impossible to inspire. Or almost impossible. Perhaps it had been those years spent in the Templeton schoolroom that had given her hope, that tiny pinprick of hope that could never be extinguished, and that made her, during the good years, a teacher of very exceptional patience and finesse.

For Hester and Lizzie had always seemed bored and restless and she had watched their disinterest with amazement, observing that nothing seemed to whet their appetite to discover and explore. She had listened to them reading too; had heard them recite, without animation or involvement, poems and plays and histories that could move her, by their tragedy or power or beauty, to wonder and to tears. Had she not known them so well she would have dismissed them as wholly unresponsive, and with them would have been discarded the many girls who followed in their footsteps, turning impassively from the jewels she displayed for their delight. But she *had* known them well. She had seen how birth, how regeneration, could make Lizzie glow with emotion, how her bedroom was full of germinating seeds and hatching frogspawn and white mice monotonously reproducing their kind. She had known that the transience of life was plain to her very early, that her love of growing things had made her unusually aware of dissolution, and that for a time she had become quite withdrawn and abstracted as she tried to unravel the meaning of these mysteries. Lizzie might have been . . . What? A biologist? A geneticist? Or perhaps, at the other end of the spectrum, a student of theology? Now nobody would ever discover, for the promise had remained hidden and had long ago rusted away to nothing, since even astute Miss Beasley had failed to detect where it lay.

Then take Hester, outwardly the most negative of pupils: what a flame of unfocused ambition had been smouldering in Hester! Somehow it could have been tended and fed, redirected and turned outwards: who could tell what she might have achieved if she had found a suitable objective for all that energy? And Victor? But the thought of Victor in his youth must be avoided for the moment. It always produced vivid pictures that seemed quite unreasonably painful, for the images were not distressing in themselves: Victor neat in his new naval uniform; Victor high in a tree, picking apples; Victor greeting the dogs, bending forward with his hands extended to caress; and now Victor swimming, emerging dripping from the water, shaking his head with such vigour that the flying drops soaked her dress . . . Yet how foolish to grieve for the past when the present was here for the taking. In a short time she would be at Coombe with Victor, and what more could she ask than that? With a conscious effort she dismissed her daydreams, and found that the car had miraculously reached the river and that she had already passed the big pool where she and Victor used to swim. She would soon be approaching Abbot's Corner. What a very loud noise the water was making this morning! She changed gear resolutely to compensate for her earlier inattention, and swung into the final bend that led to the bridge.

She was not aware of braking. In fact, when she tried to reconstruct the few vital seconds that followed she found she had no recollection of doing or thinking anything at all. Yet she must have stopped the car and even switched off the engine, for here she was sitting in safety and in silence, with her front wheels only a few yards away from the abyss. For a long time she remained motionless, wondering if perhaps she had been injured. It might be wrong to hope so, and yet somehow an injury would be dramatic enough to provide her with a diversion. It would stop her seeing, stop her caring what had happened to the bridge. She moved stiffly and cautiously, waiting for pain to grip her, but after a moment she realised it would not come. Her feet and hands were like ice, and her shoulder hurt where the safety belt had bruised it, but such trifling discomforts provided no refuge from reality. She was perfectly all right: even the red straw hat, so floppy and ill-balanced, remained secure upon her head. Very slowly she opened the door, and clinging to the bodywork, edged her way round to the front of the car.

The bridge hung in ruins, already half damming the river so that on the far side it thrashed angrily along the narrowed passage as if through an open weir. Above it the parapet still stood firm, jutting out unsupported over the rush of water and bearing the road upon it until it ended abruptly in a jagged edge of rubble and broken stone. The sharp morning light picked out the damage in aggressive detail: the newly exposed mortar flashed white along the line of the wreckage and the split bricks gaped garishly orange, their unweathered centres exposed to the sun. The crudity of the colours made the debris seem more shocking and yet curiously unreal. It was almost impossible to believe that the whole disaster was not fabricated, that she was not being deluded by some menacing *trompe l'oeil*.

At her feet lay the remnants of the fractured buttress and she bent forward and touched the nearest of the boulders, recoiling at once as she felt the solid stone beneath her hand. It was real all right, the destruction, the detritus, the distorted flow of the river. The bridge was gone. The lane was rendered useless. But then it had not been used by anyone for years now, already the tarmac was cracking and the grass was pushing through. It would hardly be worth repairing.

She looked up and beyond the devastation before her, attempting to ignore the severed stump of the road, so obscenely white and orange, that seemed to leer across at her from the opposite bank. Perhaps the sight of the gates would restore her? But the gates, now she was not able to hurry towards them, looked extraordinarily aloof and far away. Beneath them she felt herself dwindle, losing all significance, all traces of belonging. They did not need, had never needed her allegiance. They were totally indifferent to her pain. The half mile that lay between them, which had been no distance at all when each second brought her nearer, now stretched interminably before her, cutting her off completely from the welcome that she craved. She would never enjoy it again; but the worst of the hurt came from knowing that it had not really existed, that she was made ludicrous by the absurdity of her suffering. And by her impotence, her lack of any status or authority. She could not rebuild the bridge, as she would have done had she been Miriam; she had no control, no power to preserve what she loved. This pathway to Coombe – she had looked on it as her own undisputed possession, but in cold reality she had no claims upon it at all. She had simply trespassed there, an inconsequential outsider too mere to be noticed by anyone, and now its destruction had banished her for good.

She put her hands over her face, pressing them against it until the frame of her glasses cut painfully into her nose. Spots of colour flickered before her eyes, black and white, merrily mockingly orange. They gathered and dispersed, zoomed together, then scattered in all directions. Even when she opened her eyes she found she could not dispel them. They danced up and down in the sunlight, converging upon her like a swarm of flies. Nauseated, she groped for the buttress and sank down upon it, putting her head between her knees. The red hat slipped forward and lay on the ground beside her, with its feathers and the chiffon scarf that bound them, floating elegantly amid the rubbish that lapped up to her feet.

She did not know how long she sat there, but the whirling motes of colour eventually seemed to lose interest in tormenting her and disappeared. A calm crept over her, an unfamiliar calm, cold and empty, remote and rather frightening. It bore no relation to content, nor even to the strange tranquillity of the early morning, and it seemed to come from outside her, rather than to generate within. Yet it settled upon her purposefully, and after a while she looked up and glanced around her, trying to gauge the extent of its protection. Could this be the peace of God, for which she had prayed so often and so vainly? But she knew it was not so: indeed there was something positively godless about this new and inexplicable detachment. She sensed it to be precarious, a final desperate throw against the invading genie, and she rose to her feet as warily as if she was wearing an armour made of glass. Nothing happened. The glass did not splinter. Perhaps she was not yet as vulnerable as she imagined?

She picked up her hat from the edge of the river and wiped

the scarf and the feathers with her handkerchief. They seemed a trifle bedraggled, but no doubt they would look much better when they were dry. Besides it was not important. Indeed, it was suddenly plain to her that nothing much was important – not her ruined career, not the loss of Humphrey's friendship, nor the fact she must care for Father right through to the end. And the bridge, after all, what did it really matter? Nothing mattered at all, except, of course, for Victor. Only Victor counted. Victor's well-being and his happiness.

She scrambled up to the car and backed it around the corner, reversing unsteadily up the winding road. She was very bad at reversing, and the thought of two miles with no turning space would normally have left her faint with apprehension, but now she had done with all that sort of nonsense. It was tiresome to have to drive so slowly and her neck ached from craning constantly over her shoulder, but otherwise the undertaking was of no consequence any more. Nothing mattered, except for Victor, and very soon she would see him.

In the village she swung the car round to face the main road, and set off again towards the gates of Coombe.

11

The train was late, and Victor who had arrived punctually to meet it, walked once or twice up the empty platform and then retired despondently to his car. He would sit and wait, no point in going home again. He felt illogically irritated with Dickie, though of course it was quite unreasonable to blame him for the delay. Or for being on the train at all, since he himself had suggested that he should use the railway as usual; it had seemed a much better idea than inflicting him on one of the other guests. He had also insisted, in a mood so far removed from his present one that it seemed to belong to another existence, that he should go instead of Miriam to meet the train. 'It will only upset you,' he had said, 'and I so want your day to be happy.' And Miriam, apparently touched by his consideration, had not protested at all. But had she been touched? Or had she simply been treating him like a chauffeur? Ever since last night he felt he no longer knew anything about her, though no doubt that too was ridiculously unfair. He had made no opportunity yet to talk to her as he could have done, as he should have done when he got in last night. Instead he had snatched a couple of hours sleep in his dressing room and gone down to the stables again before she wakened, to speak to the lads and make arrangements for the mare.

By the time he came back she had joined the family at breakfast, and Justin had obviously explained his absence to them all. A discreet air of sympathy hung about the table, the boys leapt up politely when he entered and hastened to see he had sugar, milk, marmalade; Hester poured out his coffee, and fresh toast appeared on the instant, and William, well-known for the way he appropriated the papers, immediately offered him the *Financial Times*. Of course no one actually mentioned the misfortune, for the fact that he would be suffering discomfiture was tacitly understood. Only Miriam would have broached so delicate a subject, and Miriam did not even look up when he came in.

He rubbed his hand over his face. He should long ago have made things up with Miriam. Why had he tried to avoid confronting her? It became more clear every moment that Justin must be a liar, or alternatively that he had misread the implication of what the fellow had said. You wouldn't know what to expect of him, and besides they had both been exhausted and disappointed. Looking back he realised that the man was probably hysterical, and that in his own overwrought state he had taken the whole thing up wrong. Thank goodness he'd had the common sense not to challenge such an impossible insinuation; it was unthinkable that he should be suspicious of such a disgusting thing.

He pushed the seat back a little and straightened his legs with an indignant grunt. By God, he was stiff! Must have got badly out of condition; he seemed to have strained all the muscles in his back. And how tired he felt; but then after all, he'd been up all night and he was no longer a youngster. Not like Justin. Justin and Miriam . . . He heaved himself upright; he really must pull himself together. All this brooding was very unlike him, he could usually make his mind blank whenever he chose to do so, or just drop off to sleep. But there did not seem much hope of that this morning, he wished that he'd brought the paper with him to read. Perhaps there would be something among all that stuff in the pockets? He took out a pile of road maps and began to thumb restively through them, staring at the covers as if by some miracle 'Inner London and Bus Routes' might suddenly become his morning *Times*. What a mess! He kept meaning to throw out some of the old ones, but he never actually did so; he supposed that some foolish nostalgia was standing in his way. Here was Florence, where they'd honeymooned at Miriam's insistence, and a dog-eared Dordogne with Gaston's château marked; and Scotland in large scale, so useful if one slipped up for the shooting, though with Miriam's attitude to blood sports it hardly seemed worth the journey any more. His Scottish friends passed harsh judgement, and their standards were much more unyielding than his neighbours'. Besides there were plenty of good shoots nearer home.

He stuffed the whole bundle back again with sudden indignation, and picking up Miriam's *A to Z* which had slipped to the floor beside him, replaced the piece of paper she was using to mark her place. He saw that it was a shopping list and his eye roved over it vaguely. 'Cake' it said. 'Hairdresser, Harrods.' He smiled for the first time that morning, wondering what she had got this time in Harrods, but there was no mention of that. Only various domestic items. Cereal. Coffee. Cat Food. He put the list back and shut the book automatically, aware at the same moment that he could hear the train.

The coaches had stopped by the time he got back to the barrier, and he hurried across the footbridge cursing himself for a fool. Dickie had missed the station more than once since he lost his licence, and he should have been over there long ago, ready and waiting to extract him from the train: there had been an unpleasant occasion when Miriam had failed to find him, and they'd had to telephone through to Salisbury. He broke into a run, but as he reached the platform he caught sight of his father-in-law among the thinning crowd. Well, thank heaven for that! For a moment a lifetime of greeting friends and relations made the situation seem relatively normal, and he hastened forward and saluted him warmly, with his usual friendly and good natured smile.

"Well, Dickie! It's good to see you! Darned train always seems to be late."

As he stooped to pick up the luggage (Why a suitcase? How long was he staying?) he received an exuberant thump across his shoulders, and straightened again to receive the unwelcome embrace.

"Great to see you too, Victor! And where is my little lady?" His eyes scanned the empty platform. "Far too busy for me, I'll be bound."

Victor winced. 'My little lady.' You forgot, perhaps mercifully, most of Dickie's expressions, but they seemed to get more unbearable the longer you had him around.

"She'd have come," he began untruthfully, "but the trouble was that the baby ..." He paused in surprise as Dickie punched him playfully on the arm.

"The baby!" he cried, and he winked at him lewdly and broadly. "Nothing quietens them down like a baby! Get them breeding as soon as you can." He sniggered. "But I don't need to tell you that, do I? Didn't waste any time, did you lad?"

Victor turned away with distaste. He really could not cope with Dickie's sallies, that sort of smut had always left him cold; in fact, it left him angry. It made even his passion for Miriam into something coarse and crude.

"Let's get on," he said stiffly, returning to the suitcase. "We don't want to start the day by running late."

Dickie did not move, he seemed suddenly to have crumpled, and looking at him Victor felt himself relent. Poor old buffer, he couldn't help it. His appalling humour was only an effort to be friendly, and naturally he had hoped that Miriam would come. Well, he knew just how he was feeling now he'd started to doubt his own welcome.

"Come on," he said more warmly. "She'll be worried if we are late. And she's very anxious to see you." He lied badly and felt himself flushing with the effort, but Dickie did not seem to notice, and his expression brightened at once.

They climbed the staircase in silence with the suitcase clinking ominously between them. Victor hauled it along with annoyance, had he brought a whole crate of it down? Did he think they would run out of whiskey – at Coombe, where the cellar was famous? He glanced round at him affronted, and then realised that he had certainly been drinking on the train. Though he wasn't drunk, not by a long way. It was sad to reflect that he really preferred him plastered, it made the effort of communication a great deal less of a strain. One drunk was much like another, and you knew where you were when a fellow was incapable, a lot of his friends had a weakness in that respect. Though of course any gentleman knew there were times and places, not even Patsy would get sozzled at this sort of family affair. He sighed: all the same, Dickie sober was definitely a worse embarrassment; his manner was too familiar, his jokes were always just wrong. No one ever knew how to treat him, with no shared background and no mutual interests, though that would have been no problem if he'd been what he seemed to be. One coped admirably with one's bookie, or one's builder or one's agent, and look at all the committees one was constantly asked to chair. Good families were brought up to speak agreeably to such people, and if they happened to come to your house on business, you occasionally gave them a snorter in the office and attempted to put them at their ease. But to face them as relations was quite another matter, and Dickie, as Miriam's father, left everybody at a loss.

As he settled him into the Volvo he remembered rather grimly that at first he had hardly credited the relationship himself. A man so ill-bred, a man so gross and boorish . . . and the marriage to Cousin Grace had gone awry. Perhaps she had taken a more presentable lover? But that had just been an essay in wishful thinking, these days he could see the resemblance plainly enough. In fact, where before he had managed to ignore it, he now found that it upset him more and more. He hated to see his wife's lips, lips that seduced him by their very innocence, reproduced in coarse caricature on this hulk of a man. And her eyes, with the thick fringe of lashes – they were startling even on Dickie, but they looked alarmingly foreign away from her fair skinned face. Not the eyes for a man, he hoped Jamie would escape them; he did not want his son to look like that. He glanced down at Dickie. What was it they all used to call him in the days when he first was married to Cousin Grace? The Italian Waiter. A name chosen aptly by William, who had never been short of a suitably cutting phrase. Though William had stopped saying things of that nature lately, there was awkwardness now where companionship once reigned; a restraint, a mistrust, his own pride, William's disapproval, a breach that was widening steadily day by day.

He slammed the door angrily: must do his best on this journey. After that he could probably keep out of Dickie's way.

"Did you get some breakfast?" he said to him politely, though he had seen no restaurant car as he passed the train.

"Never touch it," said Dickie. "Leave that to young lads like you, Victor." And he suddenly flashed him a look that was full of spite. "Constitution's ruined. Washed up. Broken down by prison. Funny sort of justice that leaves a man like that. No friends, no cash, and his constitution ruined. And all for some bloody technicality . . ."

Victor let him drone on, he grew angry if interrupted, and besides he was trying to track down a thought of his own; an elusive worry, in some way connected with breakfast. It would come to him in a minute, it was just in the back of his mind.

"Rotten luck!" he said vaguely. "But maybe we'll tempt you with something. A cup of coffee, and some of Scottie's buns."

He paused. That was it, it was something to do with coffee. Cereal. Coffee. Cat food. Why was Miriam buying all that sort of stuff? Even at home Scottie handled the grocery shopping, and besides, in London, she had been staying at her club. Had some chum sent her out to buy cereal and cat food? Well, why not? He must stop himself being so possessive. It was not his business to query what shopping she had done.

"We'll be quite a small party," he said rather desperately. If he did not keep talking he felt that his reason might fail. "Just the family really, the Godparents and a few neighbours. There'll be about forty staying on to lunch."

Dickie did not reply, but once started he rattled on firmly. "Lizzie's coming," he said, "and she's bringing the whole of her tribe. I hope it's not going to be trying, but we've had to ask Aunt Eleanor. Family duty. You know the sort of thing? You see Jamie's her first great-grandchild . . ."

Not trying, by God! It was going to be bloody trying. She and Dickie had never exchanged a civil word. As a son-in-law he had pained her beyond expression, and once Grace had finally left him, she had never been heard to refer to him again.

Poor old girl, you could hardly blame her. The match had made her a laughing stock, and because she had been so ambitious for Grace's beauty the laughter had not been kind. He had thought that his marriage to Miriam might prove a consolation, but to judge by her frigid demeanour it had done nothing of the sort. And it must be admitted that Miriam made no effort to be pleasant, for naturally her loyalties lay with Dickie and the never-mentioned Grace.

"How's Gracie?" said Dickie beside him, and he looked round at him in amazement. Had he spoken aloud? No, of course not, it was just a coincidence. But how tactless of the fellow, when you thought of the life he had lead her . . .

"Pretty bad," he said coldly. "They don't think she's going to get better." After all, he had asked for it, dragging her up like that. Grace's plight was both sad and degrading; it was hard enough, even with Miriam, to discuss the health of a woman who had been killing herself for years.

"Poor old Gracie," said Dickie. "You know that they won't let me see her? I've asked at the hospital over and over again. They say she doesn't want me. But it's not true. They never tell her." His voice rose and he lurched towards Victor. "It's your bloody snooty family that's keeping me away!"

Victor swallowed. The man was uncivilised, so crass that his insults could not be taken seriously, but he looked all set to do him an injury or make him crash the car. He would tell him then, straight from the shoulder.

"Look Dickie," he said, "no one's keeping you from the bedside. Except perhaps the doctors – she's got very weak, you know. But she doesn't want to see you. I assure you she's constantly said so." He paused; this was really dreadful. He had better sugar the pill. "She isn't herself," he added, "so don't take it to heart, there's a good chap. It doesn't mean anything really. She gets queer ideas in her head."

"Queer ideas?" shouted Dickie threateningly. "Ideas you've all put there for her? 'Dickie'll wheedle you out of your money, the way he's always done. He's a con man. Don't let him near you . . .'"

Victor interrupted him icily. "Grace has got no money, Dickie. You squandered that long ago."

"*I* squandered it? How about Gracie? She certainly knew how to spend it. Every penny I earned – what a woman!" He punched his fist into his palm. "And she knew how to live! Christ Jesus! Not like all you stuffed shirts in the country. Never known how Miriam stands it, though of course she's hard as nails. Like her mother, my little lady," he spoke musingly now, more in sorrow than in anger. "What a price! Can't think how she stands it. Stuffed shirts, the lot of you."

He lapsed into a gloomy silence, he seemed to have forgotten Victor. And Victor himself remained speechless. What could anyone possibly say? The whole situation was monstrous, and Dickie half pickled already, he would soon drink himself into a stupor as he did pretty well every day. It was fatuous to listen, let alone be upset by his ravings. Hard as nails. Can't think how she stands it. Stuffed shirts, the lot of you. The man was an alcoholic. He was sick. Bitter. Lonely and jealous. The speedometer crept up to eighty as he reached the wall of the demesne.

'What a price.' Why did he say that? What the hell did he think she was buying? Was he so steeped in sordid dealings that he looked upon marriage like that? And even from such a base viewpoint, it was Miriam who had everything to offer: her youth and her beauty, the rapture her presence brought him, the enchantment she cast on each moment of his life. He had never felt so impoverished as when he paid court to Miriam, had never been more astounded than when she accepted his hand – and had shown that she loved him with frankly erotic fervour; he had not thought he had it in him to rouse passion of that degree. But rouse it he had, how could anybody doubt it? How could anyone, seeing her with him, deny that she loved him too?

He breathed more slowly: no one had ever said so. Even Ian, Lizzie's husband, had not dared to hint at that. In fact he had seemed incoherent; they had only made him their spokesman because, unlike Hester and William, he had no heritage at stake. It would have been tricky for William, with his obvious vested interest, but it still made him smile when he thought of his hapless replacement, sent down alone to beard him *faute de mieux*. A rattling good sort Ian, a fantastic shot and enormously sought after, but it had to be admitted that his grasp of ideas was not wide. Nor could you overlook the way he always stared at Miriam, his words carried no conviction when you saw the desire in his eyes. He'd have given his right hand to have her, not to marry perhaps — the thought would have terrified him, but to bring a dimension of glamour to the confines of his life. She was a great girl, Lizzie, and a simply splendid mother, but flirtation and sensuality were not her form at all.

The thought of Ian revived him. He felt suddenly younger, stronger. And what a speed he was going, he was worse than Miriam! But when he caught up with Dorothy who was just turning into the gateway, he felt a twinge of impatience at the thought of slowing down. He would have to keep behind her, and he wanted to get home quickly; he would make it up with Miriam and the day could begin afresh. What luck that the storm had blown over, it was really a beautiful morning, and here in the sheltered parkland the maples were still at their best. Round the lake their reflections were perfect, and the swans sailed placidly on the gold and russet water: he would have derived some pleasure from showing it even to Dickie, but Dickie had fallen sideways and seemed to be asleep.

As the house came in view he leant eagerly out of the window. He could see the Range Rover already disgorging its load. "Hey, you chaps!" he waved cheerfully. Grand to see Lizzie's contingent, which seemed larger than any one car could comfortably hold. He jumped out laughing and waded through luggage and children, fending off the dogs that thronged round him as best he could.

"Dear Liz! This is lovely!" He squeezed her shoulders lightly. "Dogs and sprogs all in order? Down Jasper! He's licking her face." He plucked his niece up from the gravel. "He's just pleased to see you, Flavia!" A sweet little thing, Lizzie's youngest, but she whined a lot these days.

"She was sick on the way," said Lizzie. "I expect that's why she's crying. Shut up, Flavia! Jasper loves you. Go and help Daddy empty the car." She pushed the child irritably from her. "She's so nervous. Can't think where she gets it. But how is the baby, Victor?" And her whole expression changed. She looked softer, almost youthful; little Lizzie, his favourite sister. "Utter bliss? I can't wait to see him. What a lucky old thing you are! They're so scrumptious when they're babies. You've got years of it before you." She looked round disconsolately at her own growing offspring. "How I wish one could keep them tiny, they're so difficult later on. Such a worry. Just look at Fiona!" She caught her sleeve and Fiona looked at them warily; a pale girl, with her father's lank hair falling over her forehead, and a narrow foxy face.

"Broken collar bone," said her mother. "Means she won't be able to hunt till after Christmas." And Victor saw that the child was strapped up like a hunchback, and also that the wary manner concealed dark mutiny.

"Poor Fiona." He smiled at her kindly. "Mustn't get in a fret about it. You'll still have the rest of the season. The odd broken bone soon mends."

"I hate hunting!" muttered Fiona. "And Mummy knows that I hate it. But she always tells people I love it." She glanced away and then added, clearly and rudely, "I expect she tells lies because she's ashamed of me."

Ian's shout broke the strain of the awkward moment that followed, most mercifully intervening before any more could be said. "Why, here's Miriam!" he cried gladly. "And Aunt Hester and Uncle William. Come on, gang, where are your manners?" And he urged his family forward with surprising resolution, as though he was controlling an unruly pack of hounds.

Victor looked up thankfully. Here indeed was Miriam. He had feared, and how unjustly, that she might ignore her guests;

but instead, to his pride and pleasure, she ran down the steps poised and smiling, kissing Lizzie and embracing Ian with exactly the right mixture of decorum and good cheer. She was wearing a dress of bright striped Indian cotton, very loose, very flowing; for some peculiar reason it gave the impression that she was naked underneath. As he watched, she scooped up Flavia, who was snivelling quietly beside her, and in a charmingly maternal manner, placed her upon one hip. It was not, as he had seen it before, at all a provocative posture; dear Lizzie had been straddling her young on her hip bone for years. But with Miriam, wearing that garment, the child's weight immediately brought her whole figure into prominence, crushing the thin material against thigh and waist and breast. He stared at her like any schoolboy, transparent with appraisal, and she swept across to him laughing, and casually patted his cheek.

"Wake up, darling! Just look at Ian. He's humping all the luggage!" She turned to Lizzie with a small rueful smile. "He's been up all night at the stables," she added in a low voice, "and then he rushed off to the station to meet my poor old Pa."

'Poor old Pa.' Not 'my Dad', as she always discordantly called him. She is acting, thought Victor, startled. She is simply playing a part. The affection, the charm, the good manners; she is not at all pleased to see Lizzie or the children. There is nothing about her behaviour that is honest or comes from the heart.

The thought was electrifying, its implications infinite; the instinct for self-preservation urged him to put it away. He would not watch her; he would not doubt her integrity, just because for once he had caught her in a childish little play. He had never before regarded her as an actress. He refused to imagine her sentiments might be feigned; or her passion affected, a consciously planned performance. Her innocence a deception. Her responses insincere. He would not form part of her audience, as if he too was meant to be deluded. As perhaps he had been deluded, time and time again?

Yet his feet did not move, and his eyes remained fastened

upon her: and he knew the production was practised, and very neatly staged. And doubt and fear and anger rose together and seethed within him, challenging every standard, invading every certainty, and deriding all the values that he had ever held.

12

There had once been a Norman chapel on the hillside behind the manor, and in the drought of summer, when the coarse grass was burnt and the bones of the meadows rose up where the earth had shrunk and crumbled, you could still trace its small square skeleton among the graves. The old tombstones had been gathered up and lined along the bank on the north side of the churchyard: their inscriptions had long ago been eroded, and the lichen grew upon them, splashing their rough blank faces with patches of saffron and brown. The named graves laid out before them all marked the resting places of the Templetons, for over three centuries lords of the land and the manor; and the seventeenth-century chapel had been built and endowed for the use of the family too. As a child it had quite disturbed Dorothy to think that another older church had stood there, independent of the Templetons, owing nothing to their power or patronage. Even now the idea seemed impertinent, at variance with their obvious air of ownership, their possession of soil and brick and mortar, the presence of their name on every monument and tomb. In epitaph, plaque and memorial you could follow the family history, from the time of the restoration down to the present day: a continuous record of service and prosperity, solid, judicious and authoritative; sometimes ignoring, always emerging unaffected from whatever change and turmoil shook the years.

Through succeeding generations the chapel continued to draw the family together; it was not large enough for weddings, but birth and death could always be depended upon to fill it yet again with Templetons. For Dorothy, these occasions held a personal significance; they stood out in her memory like milestones, marking and dividing the stages of her life. Yet she knew that the recollections both belittled and reproached her, underlining her exclusion from the intimate family circle, and making her thoughts turn inwards in a very self-centred way. She had given no thanks, for instance, at the service for Lady Alice, though her death had been sudden and peaceful and a merciful end to years of suffering; instead she had sat ungrateful and desolate, overcome by the knowledge that his mother's release would mean the end of Victor's compassionate posting, that inevitably he would soon go back to sea. While at Jamie's funeral, so tragic and untimely, she had found herself burdened with a still greater sin. In the midst of the family grief (which still returned to haunt her: Victor's father, bent, ailing, and stupefied by his loss; Lizzie, heavy with child, breaking down and openly weeping; her own father's hand shake as he made the sign of the cross): in the midst of their grief, and despite her real compassion, her whole being had been overflowing with entirely selfish joy. For Victor had been restored to her, and beside that miracle sorrow had dimmed and faded, like a candle flame exposed to the blaze of the sun.

She had vowed from the start that this baptism would be different. It would exorcise all the memories that could only bring her shame: the burials where she had daydreamed, the christenings where profound despair had claimed her, the pain of not really belonging, of being placed, by some subtle but rigid definition, just beyond the pale. This time Victor had redeemed her; she had been invited in, accepted, her special relationship with the family publicly recognised.

Yet just when reality offered complete fulfilment, it seemed to skim over her, eluding her grasp. She prayed for strength and serenity that she might throw off the strange confusion; it was vital to keep her mind receptive and aware. Every instant must be savoured, absorbed to the full, and then committed to memory. This morning, above all mornings, her impressions must not be lost.

Already she knew she had wasted a good half hour of pleasure. Since the Godparents had assembled her thoughts were running uncontrollably astray. The image of the bridge refused to leave her, blurring her powers of perception in a most disappointing way. She would have felt better if Victor had listened to her, for she felt that though nobody used it, some barrier should be placed across the lane. But of course there was no real urgency, it could wait until after the party; it would have been foolish to bother him when he seemed so distracted and grim. Besides his curtness had shocked her, and the fear of increasing his ill humour had stopped her approaching him again. On the whole she had felt rather better when she saw that his discourtesy was general, though it was so entirely unlike him that she wondered if he was unwell. As a host, he had been barely civil when Justin had come up to tell him that a telephone call from London had summoned him away: she had heard him explain that his understudy had been injured in rehearsal, that he must forgo his holiday and dance the part tonight, that he'd leave straight after the service – but Victor had looked at him blankly, and had not even said he was sorry that his visit was being curtailed. Perhaps he had felt it fortuitous; though it seemed unkind to show it, she herself had a guilty feeling that it might be for the best. He did rather spoil the ambiance, since the Godparents made such a very distinguished party: Patsy Braithwaite and Lord MacKenzie (whom she must call Alistair), and Bunny Montmorency, and Hester who, rather stiffly, had agreed to stand as proxy for Miriam's actress friend.

And yet she had not revelled fully in this privileged walk to chapel: she should have reaped more satisfaction from belonging to such exclusive company. Instead she had trailed behind them, tied by reluctant charity to Justin, to whom the rest of the party appeared to have little to say. Of course they had barely met him, while she had known them for years now: it was odd how Patsy and Bunny found it hard to recall her name. Victor usually helped them through this, 'Hey, Bunny! Remember Dorothy?', and then Bunny would nod recognition in her absent-minded way. But this morning he had not bothered, had not hoisted her through the stockade of their conversation; had not, though he must have seen her, even greeted her when she arrived. At the time that had hurt her deeply, but how could she doubt his affection? It was manifest before everyone that she led the chosen today. All the others were waiting for them. And here at last was the baby, whom Miriam and Nanny had decided to bring by car. She glanced round the circle of faces, smiling brightly at no one in particular, and nervously pushed her glasses higher up the bridge of her nose.

It was not until she saw Nanny bustling through the narrow wicket that it struck her she had never carried such a tiny infant before. Would she be impossibly awkward? Would he cry when he felt her stiff and inexperienced? She did not even know how to support his head. And that beautiful robe, starched and goffered, that poured down smoothly over his nurse's forearm, how could she both hold a baby and preserve its immaculate folds? It was clear that she should have practised. Why had she not thought of it sooner? How could she have reached this moment so hopelessly unprepared?

Her hands grew damp and her glasses misted over, but she had no time to wipe them and no room to turn away. The little porch was crowded, Bunny and Hester blocked the entrance, and behind her in front of the flyscreen, Victor, Patsy, Alistair. As the blur that she knew must be Nanny bore down the path towards her, she involuntarily stepped backwards and found herself tightly wedged. They were large men, especially Patsy, and they loomed above her like gaolers, their suits rasping harshly against her, nauseating her with their faint but terrible smell; an aroma of large warm bodies, wool cloth and pipe tobacco, and that unmistakable pungence that meant they had recently shaved. She was trapped, just as Humphrey had trapped her; she was stifling, trembling choking. She swayed forward, pushing past Hester, and reached the open air. She almost bumped into Miriam, and she stood and stared at her, panting. It took quite a few seconds to recognise her properly, and still longer to calm herself sufficiently to see that she was holding out her child.

"Don't you want to take him, Dollie?" That was Victor, just

behind her; and Miriam answered directly, conveying to Dorothy the curious impression that although she was standing between them, she did not exist at all.

"Let's go in," she exclaimed impatiently. "Can't you see that she doesn't want him? If you must stick to all these conventions, then I'll give him to Bunny to hold."

The words revived Dorothy, immediately and unpleasantly, as though a jug of cold water had been suddenly dashed in her face. To Bunny. The thought was unbearable. She leapt forward and snatched at Miriam, her hand dragging at the fingers that were splayed behind the baby's head.

"Give him to me!" she cried peremptorily. "Give him to me at once. I am waiting." All the hesitance of the morning had fallen away from her voice. Her manner was that of the classroom, and she held out her arms commandingly; and Miriam, though she looked startled, responded at once to the tone.

"Well, don't drop him," she said. "He's quite heavy." But she knew she would not drop him. She would not hold him clumsily either, nor destroy the sweep of his robe. From the moment her arms went round him an instinctive grace possessed her. She knew how to place his body, how to prop up his fragile head; in the crook of her arm, pressed against her, her left hand encircling his shoulder, her right hand supporting his bottom and taking the weight of his legs. The position was wholly natural. Had she spent all her life nursing babies she could not have felt more at home. He strained at her breast and she hugged him, lulled into a trance by the sweetness of the sensation, so that when Victor tapped her shoulder she could hardly remember why she was standing there: but the lapse lasted only an instant, it all flooded back as soon as he took her elbow and turned her round again to face the door. "All set?" he said, bending over her; and when she nodded confidently, they entered the chapel together with the rest of the party clustering behind. How extraordinary to feel them there, to know she was leading them in, alone with Victor and Jamie! What deeper pleasure, what greater satisfaction could she ever have expected the day to hold?

But still between her and her felicity there lay an unearthly detachment, a light-headed feverish feeling that she was outside and above the whole affair. The warmth of the baby against her simply added to the illusion, for the sensual thrill of clasping him was one that she had only known in dreams. And the presence of Victor beside her, how often had she imagined it? Years of make believe, scores of pretended situations floated and mingled together in her head. She was stately and gracious, and elegant in a hat that crowned her beauty; but no, that was just the old fairytale, she knew she was awkward and plain, and moreover was wearing a hat that emphasised her lack of bearing and reduced her appearance to absurdity. She looked down, and felt some small comfort that at least it pleased the baby; he was staring transfixed at the feathers and crumpled chiffon that hung like a nursery mobile above his face. She nodded her head for him, watching his eyes as they strove to focus on the movement, touched by the way his small hands wavered towards it, feeble and unco-ordinated, clasping and unclasping although there was nothing there for him to hold. He was so exceedingly helpless: the desire to cherish and protect him seized her suddenly with a violence that was sharper than physical pain. Victor's baby. Her baby. Their baby. What a terrible thought, senseless, wicked! God forgive me, she prayed. God release me. Give me grace to enjoy this moment as it is in reality.

She tore her gaze from the baby, though it was not easy to do so; but if she asked Him to help her, she must try to play her part. Her glance fell at random on Lizzie, poor Lizzie who lately seemed shrewish and discontented; she saw now that for her this same craving had acquired the lure of a drug. All those babies, so briefly fulfilling, kept increasingly long sucking bottles and wearing nappies, and finally roughly rejected as soon as their drawn-out infancy was done. Well, that would not happen to Jamie. Victor would be the best of fathers. There was no reason to doubt that both his parents would offer him steadily increasing love. She must place much more faith in Miriam, after all she had always respected Victor's judgement and his knowledge of Miriam's character was far greater than her own: besides (with God's strength she must face it), her initial assessment had been warped by envy, and all her impressions tainted by the onset of her breakdown. She had been ungenerous, critical; in her ignorance she had formed insensitive judgements. Without charity we are nothing; and she had been empty of charity, the blackest emptiness of all. She must pray that in His vast mercy He would fill her with His charity, that pure and exacting virtue that seeketh not even its own: that thinks no evil; that bears, believes, endures all things that are sent to try it; and with a supremacy far beyond her imagining, is never known to fail.

She bowed her head meekly and shut her eyes against distraction, relieved that her face was hidden by the droop of the hat's huge brim. Perhaps He had guided her wondrously towards its strange selection, first to humble and then to reward her with the gift of privacy? Behind the hat, in seclusion, she could go through the whole epistle, and somewhere along the journey He would touch her with heavenly grace. Then she would be at peace again, renewed in her faith that one day she would find Him; that before Him, pardoned and shriven, she would revel in all that she loved. 'For now we see through a glass darkly.' She shuddered: how dark the glass, how impenetrable; how empty the void where the shadowy face must linger, how frail her own courage to trust its obscurity. She could only hope, when she reached the words in context, that their promise might yet bring her comfort. 'For now we see through a glass darkly; but then face to face.'

But she had no time, they would not let her finish. She felt Victor's hand on her elbow, heard the rector murmuring them closer to the font. So keen was her frustration that she almost resisted the summons, but the blessed epistle saved her from such a selfish excess. Charity does not behave itself unseemly; is not easily provoked. She stepped forward, clutching Jamie, and with her heart full of contrition, looked straight across at Miriam who was standing beside Justin on the opposite side of the font.

A narrow beam of sunlight fell through the chancel window, striking the brass plaque above them so that it exploded into flame. Beneath it, full in the spotlight, they blazed fluorescent together, their bright clothes brighter, their fair heads fairer, brashly vivid and colourful against the restful gloom. For a moment, startled and dazzled, she felt nothing but tenderness for them. They looked so brittle and vulnerable; their very flamboyance seemed pathetically defiant, as if they were determined to flaunt the fact that they were out of place: a pair of brilliant butterflies who had fluttered down by accident, blown to a hostile climate from a lush and tropical land.

Dearly beloved. A pair of brilliant butterflies. For as much as all men are conceived and born in sin. A pair. She stiffened, appalled by the image that assailed her. This was Miriam, Jamie's mother; Miriam, Victor's wife. Their whole future lay in her keeping. Yet the hideous thought had the impact of revelation, a scourge that was sent to plague her as charity, thinking no evil, should be sweetly pervading her soul. None the less, she continued to watch them, watched them while charity mocked her: watched as briefly they turned to each other with a slight lift of the eyebrow, a minimal curve of the lip; saw the way that their eyes held and parted, with that bold naked look she abhorred in any context and that made her feel faint with alarm and aversion today. Still she watched, while the rector demanded that she renounce the devil, the world and its glories and trappings and the carnal desires of the flesh. It was never a pleasant passage, its crudeness seemed inappropriate at any christening, but today, sickened by suspicion, the words burnt like fire in her brain. How could Justin take this upon him, in God's house, if her fears were well founded? But his mouth moved, and by some reflex she found that she was speaking too. In a low but audible chorus, on behalf of Victor's baby, she heard them both declaring that they renounced them all.

She could not have seen it. Of course she had not seen it. But she would not risk looking at Miriam again. This service was always emotive, and the feelings the baby aroused in her had been better left undisturbed. They awoke unchaste longings, encouraged the weaving of fantasies, and no doubt this prurient conjecture was also part of their spell. She must not, she would not, believe it. As in all cases where faith was called for, she would force herself to subjugate her mind. She would disregard all the sign posts that pointed away from the path of righteous thinking, never questioning, never challenging, never probing too deep or too far. How else had she survived the Creed, that eternal interrogation? Even now she was being called upon to avow her belief anew: that her Lord was conceived by a miracle and delivered of a virgin; that his mortal remains had been physically resurrected from the tomb. Did Father believe it, conception and resurrection? The life everlasting where blessed souls basked in the Grace? His whole life professed that he did so, and she had not dared to investigate its foundations – for fear, or so she had told herself, that he would be shocked and grieved at her own sad lack of faith, and that once flawed, his pleasure in their shared devotions would never reassert itself or be complete again. But was that the reason? Or was she simply frightened? Afraid that his explanations would leave her more lost than before? Or worse, that behind his assurance she would find that he too was uncertain, that the rock of his conviction was hollow as a gourd? Had she found such a weakness in Father, life would have been insupportable; Father's certitude, Father's fervour stood between her and the dark. Father's faith and Victor's welfare. No doubt must threaten or destroy them. God existed, and He would bless Victor and shield him from all harm.

She lifted her voice with the others. How untroubled, how positive and sincere they sounded: Patsy's drawl, Ian's swallowed vowels, Alistair with his curt clipt bark; and Hester and Bunny in harmony, as if generations of breeding had honed their accents to the same cutting edge. Did she alone falter? Was she alone guilty, irresolute? She dare not look at Justin. All this I steadfastly believe.

I believe: it was always better when she had said it. I believe that no life can ever be lived in vain: that no sparrow falls unheeded; that no deprivation is without its meaning; that handicap, flood and famine are all part of His vast just plan. I believe that He gazes with pity even on my own small torments, that they also have their purpose; that I am fulfilling His will. I believe in Victor's affection. I believe in Miriam's purity. I believe He is here in this chapel, the Shepherd among his sheep.

Her heartbeats slowed as the moment of conflict receded. It was over. She was safe again. No disaster had taken place. She was limp with relief, like a fugitive whose unreliable papers have carried him past the scrutiny of a vigilant frontier guard. The ordeal done, her surroundings at last took substance; she stared greedily around her; she had been too long away. But now she was home, free to glory in its solid actuality: free to take her place calmly in the events of the day.

Expertly, she offered up Jamie to the bulge of the rector's surplice, surprised at how light her arms felt when he was gone. Light and empty. She smothered the emptiness with attention, fixing her eyes on his eggshell skull as she pronounced his name. How good to hear her own voice ring out, firm and confident with authority; to know that guilt and hesitation now lay behind her, conquered by the affirmation of her faith.

The rector sprinkled. The baby cried. Miriam smiled at Victor. Justin stirred like a man who fears he may miss his train. Through a chink in Lizzie's packed pew, she caught a glimpse of Father, his head framed reassuringly against Nurse Rose's midriff, and his hands, with the meaningless rhythm of the sick and aged, rubbing back and forth on the arms of his wheelchair. No, nothing was changed. Everything was as it should be. The affection that surrounded her was uncomplicated and wholesome, and a happy family ceremony was drawing to a close. It was obvious to her now that she had simply imagined all the undercurrents of feeling that had tortured her sensibilities earlier in the day. She must really take more care of herself, if only for Father's sake and for Victor's: it was foolish to underestimate the effect of excitement and stress. All the doctors had emphasised quiet, though each day she was getting stronger: when you paused to consider how far she had come since her breakdown, you could only be encouraged by the progress she had made. Who would have thought she would stand here, composed and at peace with her situation, if they had seen her in the hospital not so very long ago?

What a lot there was to be thankful for, faith and beauty, the warmth of friendship. It was hard to recall at this moment why life seemed so hard to bear, or why she quailed and faltered beneath the burden that He had allotted to her, forsaking Him in her iniquity as she had done last night. She would do her best to atone for it, with penitence and with sturdy resolution, and fortified by His mercy, she would vanquish despair and sin.

With her eyes closed, she knelt for the Lord's prayer. Ah, the joy of His presence, the protection of His omnipotence! The solace of crying out to Him, knowing that He would listen to the words He Himself had exhorted all men to pray. Lead us not into temptation, but deliver us from evil. Amen.

13

Coombe was made for such festivities. Through long years of conviviality its atmosphere had mellowed, so that to its elect it presented the cordial air, the warm and clannish welcome of a long established and exclusive club. Nothing brash, nothing raucous obtruded on the senses: even the brittle sunlight was tempered as it settled on the faded silk that papered the walls of the dining room. Down the long expanse of the table it glowed rich and deep on wood and glass and silver, glass that did not sparkle and silver that did not glitter, but reflected the light with the dignity of age. Here the exquisite and the ugly united without friction, blended by their surroundings into a sweet accord: the Hepplewhite chairs stood easily round the gouty Victorian table; the Chinese laquer cabinets, in a faded extravagance of gold and black and scarlet, were at peace with the Georgian sideboard that stood on the opposite wall. It was hard to imagine such furniture being purchased, to connect it with the exchange of money in any way: it seemed to spring up spontaneously from the oak beams underneath it, just as the threadbare Aubusson carpet appeared to be part of the floor. The verdicts of the market place had no bearing on its position, its quality was self-evident, its worth could never be a matter of debate. Self-assured, it simply existed, secure in the tacit assumption that whatever its age or condition it was in the best of taste.

Last night, as Dorothy had piled chrysanthemums into an urn in the corner, the shutters had been fastened and the great brocade curtains drawn against the storm. The room had been tranquil and friendly, a haven from the lightning, and she had felt quite at ease there, as if the refuge it provided had been prepared especially for her to enjoy. Now, filled with colour and clamour, its atmosphere had become impersonal, its intimacy withdrawn from her as if it had never been. It offered its hospitality with a distant condescension, and as she jostled through the doorway she felt suddenly aggrieved. After all, as a child she had lived here, for weeks and occasionally for whole terms together, when poor Mother, already suffering from multiple sclerosis, was prostrated by periods of illness and pain. Did they know about that, all these people who greeted each other across her? Did they know that time without number she had been the only guest? That she had sat among the family like an honorary relation, an accepted part of the household, the most intimate of friends? Did they realise she was special, that she was at home in this setting? How she wished she could make her relationship abundantly clear and plain! Did they know it was she who had arranged the flowers? Had they even recognised her in the church today?

In silence she began to shuffle down the table, searching for the white card that would bear her name. They were hard to read at that distance, but at last she discovered it somewhere in the middle, between Basher Montmorency on her left hand and Dickie on her right. Well she must not feel resentful, somebody had to deal with Dickie; it was probably quite a compliment to be chosen for the task, and allotted to it unaided, for she saw Lizzie's little Fiona was sitting pale and speechless upon his other side. She pulled in her chair and adjusted her spectacles firmly; she was trained to discipline children and in this condition Dickie was little more than a child; all she had to do was prevent him from any excess of bad manners, from spilling his glass, or shouting or falling off his chair. It might not make for an edifying or even a restful luncheon, but at least she could gain satisfaction from a difficult job well done.

She risked a quick glance at Basher, who might in the end prove more daunting, for despite his reputation for racy conversation, she found him surprisingly difficult company. She could not help being demoralised by the way his eyes darted round the room while she was talking, and by the unceremonious way he left her when anyone more congenial could possibly be found. Once at a cocktail party he had vanished in the middle of a sentence, so abruptly that she had finished it as she stood in the corner alone: that had made her feel very foolish, but perhaps on the whole it was better than having him here beside her, a bored and restive captive whom she could never hope to entertain. However, just now she saw she need not worry; he was happily occupied in a shouted exchange with Lofty Arbuthnot who sat hunched like a wounded heron on the opposite side of the table, with Hester and Amy MacKenzie flanking him on either hand. They were talking with great animation about the start of the shooting, and of the MacKenzies' houseparty, which she knew was an annual event: it gave rise to a multitude of stories, every raconteur had his own version, and she fixed her gaze hopefully on Lofty; if he started to reminisce she was sure to hear about Victor, who stayed with the MacKenzies each November and never failed to feature in tales about their shoot. But Lofty had not yet drunk enough to be ripe for story telling, and instead the conversation turned to William and Hester's plight; they would miss the first day altogether, and indeed if the House sat late that night, they would have to drive down to Gloucestershire in the small hours again. But they'd certainly come. Good gracious, they would drive all night if it meant getting out of London. London, remarked Hester plaintively, was getting worse every day. And really this year, in the heatwave . . .

"It's high time", interrupted Amy, "that you two stopped complaining and found yourselves somewhere down here. Everyone has a base in the country if they've got to work in London, and besides what about the horses? You'll need stabling of your own." She sniffed disapprovingly. "Anyway, who knows at the next election? And if William does scrape back again he could stay up during the week."

Hester frowned. She said that on purpose, thought Dorothy in astonishment. She must realise how upset he was when he barely held his seat. And she certainly knows that Coombe was their base until Victor married Miriam; how could William replace it with anything that he would be proud to own? He would have to be fabulously wealthy. Why had Amy sounded so pitiless? Surely her lifelong affection for Hester had not waned? It was very wrong to wonder if perhaps it had been affected by the fact that she was no longer the virtual owner of Coombe.

She looked away almost thankfully as Dickie started speaking, though at first he seemed quite contented with his own soliloquy. "Quite a palace she's got," he was saying. "Like a ruddy antique market." He lifted a wavering finger and held it in front of his face. "Fancy bit of stuff. Wouldn't mind it. Fetch a bit if you took it to Christies." He swung round upon her suddenly as if he expected a fight. "You! You don't care about that, do you? You don't care if the thing's worth thousands. That one bloody great lump of silver would see me straight for life!"

Dickie's voice was loud, and his outstretched arm quivered half across the table. Just for an instant everyone within range glanced involuntarily at the centrepiece towards which he was pointing as though its very stateliness had provoked his particular rage: a vast epergne, cumbrously fashioned in heavily ornate silver, its arms bearing swing-handled baskets of lavish rococo design. Dorothy stared at it stupidly. She had seen it, had sat beneath it, had eaten the sweetmeats it carried on countless occasions like this; and yet she had never studied it, it had simply been there like a symbol of the gracious unstinted bounty that the Templetons offered their friends. Now, in the glacial silence that followed Dickie's outburst, the epergne made a conscious impression in a way it had never done before. Its scrolled ornamental branches, festooned with medallions and vine leaves, seemed simply over-elaborate, indecently lavish and gross; and the baskets brimming with delicacies, fat raisins and sugared almonds, marron glacé and liqueur chocolates, filled her suddenly with disgust. The whole thing was decadent, profligate, it epitomised mindless gluttony; in its way it offended as deeply as the bleak and functional ugliness she endured in the school canteen. Yet it outfaced Dickie completely, for he too was vulgar and dissolute, and his challenge to its extravagance only rested on envy and spite. All at once she thought of Humphrey, his boy's club, his much patched jacket, the streak of the puritan in him that struck a reluctant chord: he would not feel at home at this table . . . But such thoughts were completely irrelevant, and perhaps disloyal to Victor who would certainly be mystified by her feelings about the epergne. To him it was just an ornament, barely noticed, familiar from childhood, though no doubt it appeared to Miriam as an emblem of success. Unconsciously she craned forward to confirm this disquieting reflection, but Miriam, sitting listlessly at the head of the table, no longer seemed to tally with it at all. She looked bored and inattentive, very far from the jubilant hostess who was revelling in putting her possessions on display. In fact, she looked strained beyond bearing. Maybe she was exhausted, burnt out by the dazzling vitality that had singled her out this morning as she stood beside the font?

She sat back as conversation broke out again around her, as concerted a sound as if someone had switched on the radio. The frigid silence was over, and the table had made its decision: both Dickie and his sentiments were unworthy of remark. The rules of the club were unbending about irredeemable misfits: they ceased to exist altogether, while you talked on over their heads. You did not invite their opinion, ask their business, or find out their interests; and if despite this, they still were rash enough to embark on their own tiresome subject, then you simply gave the impression you had not heard what they said. Most capitulated quickly, the more intelligent the victim the less likely it was that the message would be misunderstood for long. But Dickie, drunk or sober, was not sensitive to atmosphere. She must not let him spoil Victor's party by further unseemly remarks. Unfortunately, he forestalled her.

"See the old harridan with the diamonds?" He lurched over her confidentially. "That's my mother-in-law, did you know? That's Miriam's dear old Granny!" He gave a choking giggle, and pointing at Lady Eleanor, went on inexorably. "Sour old cow if ever there was one, and stinking rich into the bargain; but she'd not lift a hand to help you if you were dying at her feet. Not even her own precious daughter . . ."

"Oh hush! Please, Mr Bernstein!"

"Whasamatter? You rich too? All right then. All you rich are as mean as hell. But that bag of bones! She's pure poison." He began to laugh, waving his soup spoon. "Bet it gives the old tartar a bellyache to see me back again!"

His gestures were wild, but before she could prevent him, his spoon fell loudly and messily, splattering his Vichyssoise.

"Oh dear me, just look at the table!" She mopped at it ineffectually. At least it was some consolation that Lady Eleanor was deaf, and perhaps the spilt soup could be counted as another disguised blessing, for he seemed subdued by the incident and had sunk back on his chair. And then to her horror she saw that he was swaying, that his florid face had become unpleasantly grey. In a moment he would topple, fall forward on the table with a hideous crash of breaking china and glass: the spilt wine, the spilt blood, the undignified mess and confusion – as the prospect unfolded before her her ears began to sing with the maddening persistence that always preceded panic. (Dear God, let me keep control of myself! Oh Lord, let me not give in. Please let me stop this disaster.) She rose to her feet with the sluggishness of a nightmare, knowing she would have to touch him, support him out of the room, hold his arm, feel his weight. Surely somebody would help her? She looked at the back of Basher's bullet shaped head. He was close, he could hardly refuse her in spite of his obvious decision to ignore a disturbance that did not involve his friends. And then as her hand was raised to tap his shoulder, Victor's voice pierced the nightmare and scattered the panic away. "Hold on, Dollie. What's up with him?" God and Victor had seen her, had come to release her in this miraculous way. "Don't bother the others. I think we can slip him out quietly." The moment was private. His words were for her alone.

She looked at him, limp with gratitude. She just hoped she had acted properly, getting up from the luncheon table in that impetuous way; but as if he read her anxiety, he smiled suddenly, "Jolly good effort, you spotting the poor old rascal wasn't going to stay the course!"

After that, of course, it was wonderful, though she did feel a little guilty that her pleasure stemmed indirectly from Dickie's complete disgrace. They hoisted him up between them, and when Victor said he would fetch Harold, she turned the suggestion down with alacrity. The staff were all so busy, and Harold was serving the salmon; they could manage him together and make much less of a fuss. They would get him up the east wing stairs which were just outside the dining room, and put him in one of the bedrooms that lay immediately above.

As they mounted he clung to the bannisters, and on the outside Victor had his arm behind his shoulders to ensure that he did not fall. Dorothy hovered about them, now in front, now behind if Dickie looked like stumbling. Helping Victor in this manner made her own head feel quite light; now and then she felt so elated that she almost skipped around them, like the travesty of a child round a Christmas tree.

They rested on the landing to review the situation. They neither knew where he was sleeping, but his glazed eyes showed that any further delay would result in him finally collapsing on the carpet, frustrating all their efforts to tidy him away. It was Dorothy who noticed that the door of the nearest bedroom stood open on a room with an unmade bed but which otherwise seemed to be empty of all personal possessions. Justin's room. Of course! He had left without waiting for lunch. It was no surprise that on such a busy morning the staff had not bothered to take his linen away.

"In here!" she cried, pleased at her resourcefulness. "Justin's not coming back, there'll be no one to disturb him. We'll pop him in here and he can sleep all day."

As they jostled him through the doorway with a "Woa, steady there!" from Victor, Dickie responded quite amiably and sat down on the bed, but as he slumped back on the pillows he grew suddenly restless and fretful, glaring round him as if some menace was lurking about the room. Victor had taken his jacket and shoes, and loosened his necktie, and now he began to shiver; the day was growing cold. As Victor crossed the room to close the windows, Dorothy bent over him, trying to pull out a blanket from the wreckage of the bed. Without warning he heaved himself upright and grasped her by the elbow, drawing her closer to him and peering into her face. His eyes were uncannily empty and unfocused, yet she felt herself held by their fixed reptilian stare.

He began to mumble urgently. "A right cockup you've made, little lady. Dickie's through, but he knows a dud contract. They're going to swallow you whole. Just the way they did with poor Gracie . . ."

"I'm not Miriam," whispered Dorothy. Heaven knows what the poor man was raving about, but she felt rather glad that Victor could not hear. "Not Miriam," she repeated, wresting her arm away roughly. He fell back against the pillow, but she saw from the look on his face that he had not heard her protests; and suddenly and unpleasantly she too was aware of Miriam, aware in a positive way that owed nothing to Dickie's mutterings. It was a jarring sensation, and she felt an acute reluctance to trace it to its source.

She would not think about Miriam: she ripped the sheet off abruptly as if action would drive the unwanted presence away. Instead for a shocking moment Miriam seemed to leap towards her, flying up from the crumpled linen in front of her very face. She flailed at the apparition, and at once the thing fell limply, leaving its fragrance behind it and spreading itself at her feet. She stared at it, bathed in the aura of its perfume. Miriam's perfume. Miriam's evening shawl. Ethnic, fashionably fringed, arrestingly coloured. Unmistakably the shawl she had worn last night.

Her mind twisted to excuse it, to remain innocent of its message, to escape the implication of finding it here in this bed. Surely some explanation would come to her and protect her from the knowledge that seeped, evil and putrescent, into her consciousness? She felt she was fighting for balance on a cliff top, clawing the air for some handhold to stay her fall, the fall into filth and corruption, into faithlessness, ugliness, madness. She would grasp at anything, clutch at any straw; she would force her intelligence under as she often had done in such crises, admitting to her awareness only what could be safely born. The shawl would lose its significance, she would forget she had seen it, she had probably been mistaken in thinking it Miriam's shawl. If she blotted it out quickly, the whole episode would vanish, leaving no lasting imprint behind it on her brain.

She looked up, already halfway towards salvation, and there was Victor, staggeringly real; controverting all delusion, denying all self-deception: he existed and his betrayal existed as well. The pretence was over, the refuge had finally toppled, there remained no crack or crevice where she could hide. The full light of Victor's realness pierced the shadows, shone in the corners where the genie lay and woke him, stark and powerful, and with him the image of a profane coupling on this very bed became inescapable, as vivid and as monstrous as Father's fear of her cruelty today. Inescapable as the memory of her failure, the drugs, the electric shocks, the hospital bed; as the seething crowd in the playground; as the walls lurid with graffiti; as last night's alter ego that waited to pounce again. Inescapable. Father withered: Humphrey lost through her own deficiency. The bridge gaped and yawned, a lifeline torn apart. Rejoice in the truth; rejoice not in iniquity. But the truth was iniquity; corruption and failure and waste. Hypocrisy. Fornication. Like the victim of an earthquake she stood stunned, staring at Victor, while the house of many mansions split asunder and fell from the skies.

Nothing remained but a void. She could sense its vastness, an evil wasteland stretching without end from a present rank with duplicity and empty of all honour, into a bleak and godless eternity. An eternity in which they would all be extinguished, the arrogant and the humble, the good along with the bad.

"All set then," said Victor. "Don't think we can do much

more for him. Better get back at the double or Miriam will fret."

She could hear him through the numbness. In this new debased existence he was all that remained of integrity or beauty, of fidelity or innocence. He feared Miriam would be fretting. Somehow she would protect him from Miriam. He must not be humiliated, must not face this treachery. Means would have to be found to save him; and she would find means, for no ethics, no recognised code of principles existed in the void.

She smiled as she murmured an answer. She smiled as she covered up Dickie. She smiled as, safely protected by the height of the fourposter bed, she bent down and shoved the scented shawl out of sight beneath the valance. Victor was simple and trusting, a stranger to hate and despair. How would he guess that iniquity had invaded her like a pestilence, that faith and hope and virtue had shrivelled in her soul? He would never guess while she smiled at him. Her eyes watered, her muscles trembled with the effort. It would take all her strength to sustain it. But for Victor's sake she would smile.

14

Everyone who visited Coombe was assumed to have time to linger. Those who called for a drink often found they had stayed to dine; weekend guests appeared at the table for lunch on Mondays; friends in transit were effortlessly put up for the night. Left alone, all the Templetons spent much time in the open, and becoming easily bored, retired early to bed; but entertaining was based on more than friendship, it was a competitive yardstick of social success, and since conversation by common consent was unvaried, the yardstick was largely measured in terms of time. The successful dance ended with breakfast, in satisfying exhaustion; dinner parties proceeded doggedly into the night, and no escape was at hand for the stultified or the weary, who knew well that to slip away early was considered the poorest of form.

The sort of lunch party that followed a family christening was designed by tradition to fill the whole of the day. By the time the champagne had circulated a number of times in the drawing room, the guests never reached the table till well into the afternoon. Jamie's christening was no exception. The hours passed; the air in the dining room grew stale. The sunlight left the windows and the outside world receded, condensation crept up stealthily from the bottom of each pane.

For Dorothy, time seemed petrified. She sat quietly, alone in her limbo, between Basher's averted shoulder and Dickie's empty chair. Occasionally Basher startled her with a "More wine?" or "Jolly good venison!", but his reservoir of good manners was exhausted by such remarks. Once or twice her abstraction was punctured by small needles of conversation, "Not seen Victor up north this season?" "Out of bounds now, poor old chap." When her ears picked up these inflections, half regretful, half derisory, she felt her features harden, but mostly she managed to smile: at the mousseline of salmon, at the venison and ratatouille, the meringues and the crème brulée, the peaches simmered in wine. Extravagant food in quantities quite often nauseated her, but this food was inoffensive as an artificial display; she would as soon have eaten the plates on which it rested, but the changing courses absorbed her in an almost hypnotic way. Each collage was colourful, varied, the hours melted away as she stared at them, lost in contemplation of their texture and design.

By the time they returned to the drawing room the log fires, brightly burning, were reflected in the windows against an inky blue. Swift and sudden, the autumn darkness. Somewhere in it poor Father, exhausted, would be suffering from the painstaking ministration of Nurse Rose. Upstairs in the lamp-lit nursery, Victor's child would be feeding, bathing, oblivious of the revellers who were honouring him below. Upstairs. Upstairs too, in the room where Dickie was sleeping, an evening shawl lay crumpled under a bed. All the servants would recognise it, and any servant finding it could hardly fail to speculate on how it had come to be there. Gossip and speculation. Whispers. The rumour of scandal. The start of Victor's long landslide into suffering and disgrace, the bitter humiliation that at all costs must be avoided. She clenched her teeth: for a start, the shawl must be moved without further delay. She was here to look after Victor; she would go upstairs, who would miss her? Her coffee cup had slopped over, and with a shaking hand she put it down deliberately on one of the beautiful tables – boulle marquetry, intricate, delicate, mounted in bronze and chased with gold; not a table on which to put coffee cups, but tables no longer mattered – and felt no responsibility as she watched it steaming there.

She slipped into the hall where the fire burnt low and the dusk was heavy with shadows, but as she scurried across it towards the curving stair, the telephone shrilled in the silence and she froze between the stone pillars, as rigid with apprehension as if she was a thief. Yet why did she fear discovery? No one could guess her errand. It was senseless to cower like an animal in the middle of the hall. The telephone went on ringing. In the drawing room the roar of the party would drown its sound completely, and the staff must be out of range as they rattled about between dining room and basement. Still she hesitated, peering into the dark; but the bell was insistent, commanding; she had never ignored the telephone. A lifetime of obedience drew her slowly, against her will, and she lifted the receiver, holding it stiffly, well away from her, for some reason it seemed important that it should not touch her face. Even so, the voice reached her clearly, vibrating through her whole body, and connecting her on the instant to the blackness, to the void.

"Mrs Templeton?" Justin? Justin. "Might I speak to Mrs Templeton?" Justin's voice, redolent of evil, brought the images back again: gruesome, crude and terrifying, pressing closer, all around her; the wall began to draw inwards, the ceiling to descend. The pillars beneath the gallery were lurching towards her, swaying; like the bridge, like her faith they were toppling, and crushing her underneath.

"Can you hear me? Hello! Can you hear me? Can I speak to Mrs Templeton?" Her fingers clenched the earpiece; in a moment, perhaps she could speak, or at least replace the receiver – but already the pillars were steadying, a new power was giving her courage, a power so strong and unscrupulous that it could invade the void.

"Hello?" The voice was bewildered, then cautious, "Is that you Miriam? Look, if you can't talk freely, why not ring me back at the flat?"

The power was increasing. "I'm sorry, but you must have got the wrong number." She still gasped, but the words were coherent. "No, that's perfectly all right."

The wires whirred as he disconnected, and she stood without moving for some time, listening to the rhythmic purring of the dialling tone. The drawing room door opened, shut again; light steps clicked on the flagstones. She turned her head slowly towards them, the telephone still in her hand.

"Who's that?" said Miriam. "Dorothy? God, it's dark! I

can hardly see you." She crossed to the gaming table and impatiently snapped on the lamp. "Oh, you're on the phone! Who is it? Is it someone wanting Victor?"

Dorothy put the receiver determinedly back on its rest. "No," she said. "No. It was Justin. For you."

"Justin?" Miriam stared at her. "But you've cut him off! Why did you do that if he wanted to speak to me? Why didn't you come and get me?" Her voice was sharp with vexation, the vexation of an animal that hears a mating call and is baulked of immediate response to it. Well, you could forgive an animal.

"I'll ring him back. Where was he calling from? Did he say he was at the flat?"

"No," said Dorothy, clearly and coldly. "No. He wasn't phoning from London." She was not going to contact her lover from the shelter of Victor's hall. "He was in a phone box," she added with momentary inspiration. In a phone box you gave no number, and sometimes your money ran out. A phone box could be anywhere: as she spoke she was not expecting that her words would convey a prospect that brightened Miriam's face.

"In a phone box? You mean at the station? Did you tell him I'd come and collect him? It will only take twenty minutes," she glanced at the watch on her wrist. "I'll be back before anyone's missed me."

The station at Coombe Bassett. Although she would never have thought of it, she now saw exactly why Miriam assumed he might be there. Anyone who caught a last-minute train used the telephone booth on arrival, and a car was sent to fetch them and bring them up to the house. She had only to nod to send Miriam flying off on a fool's errand, though when she returned empty handed the nod would be hard to explain. A petty, vindictive action, of no benefit to Victor, but she let herself revel briefly in the sequence that flashed through her brain: Miriam, hot with iniquity, for once herself the victim, whirling through darkened parkland, her false expectations rising as she roared down the straight to the bridge . . . With a devastating clarity the events of the morning came back to her.

The bridge was not there. There was nothing: only a raw edge of stone. Only a broken roadway ending without warning, a lethal drop to extinction for the traveller in the dark.

"Don't just stand there gaping, Dorothy. Did Justin ring from the station?"

Her scent was heady, sickening, the smell of betrayal and sin. The smell of the shawl in the bedroom, the smell that would throttle Victor, contaminating for ever his capacity to love. Destroying his self-confidence, making him into a laughing stock, a foolish middle-aged cuckold besotted on a whore.

The power was pressing upwards: she had power over Miriam, total power of life or destruction. She could send her into the night and she would not return to them to torture them with her perfidy, to wreck Victor's life and expose him to mockery and shame. Miriam dead. The prospect had never before occurred to her. Miriam's death would bring sorrow to Victor without a doubt; but a dignified tragic sorrow in which he would be supported, solaced by the sympathy of everyone he knew. Time would heal his grief: his judgement, his faith in himself would be salvaged, and she would be here to look after him and keep him company. Coombe would be as it always had been, free from vulgarity and corruption. The power filled the void, swollen, bloated by the venom of her hate.

'Don't just stand there gaping, Dorothy.' Yes, she hated Miriam, hated her. Hated the sexuality that defiled everything in its path. Hated her smile, her beauty, her capacity to manipulate: but now it was she who was powerful. There was no mercy in the void.

"Yes. I told him someone would fetch him."

She had spoken. The words hung between them, as complete, and now as detached from her, as if they had life of their own. They had gathered their own momentum, she had no control of their consequence. If Miriam was sensible she would go by the main road. Nobody would expect her to take the short cut in the darkness. Nobody could anticipate she might go by Abbot's Bridge. And if she did? The power writhed again, half terrified, half exultant: if she went by the bridge then nobody, least of all Victor, would know where she was going, or why she had fled from the house to her own destruction. If she chose to behave so insanely, then the fault was entirely her own.

"I'll get a coat."

Dorothy waited as she darted under the pillars and came back wrapped loosely in something dark that hid her brilliant dress; a cloak as plain as a uniform, like the nurses' cloaks at the hospital, so deep and dense a navy blue that it was almost black. It certainly became her; in it she looked elfin, spectral, with her fair hair catching the firelight and framing her luminous face. Now that she saw her dispassionately, she perceived how Victor saw her, youthful, innocent, guileless, the princess in a fairy tale.

She smiled: the picture was pleasing; the lighting, the costume perfect; she was glad of the chance to appraise her as she never had done in the past. For now her beauty was harmless, purified, cleansed and shriven; a transient thing without substance that soon would exist no more.

15

Victor had never been prone to introspection. His values and his opinions had been determined from birth, and he had not paused to question them or wonder if they were changing in the forty odd years of his comfortable bachelorhood.

There was Good, exemplified largely by the qualities of his own family; and Bad, which was found to be manifest in the attitudes they deplored, anarchy, and atheism, the lack of physical courage, and all political thinking that strayed too far to the left. Good came to full flower in the country, where God's pure air and honest human toil, and above all the joys of sportsmanship, built up the body and dissuaded the mind from the dangerous process of thought. Bad flourished in cities, examples of it were numerous and horrifying, though English cities, it must further be said, had been built and strengthened by solid English backbone, and could be considered less lurid than the rest.

Somewhere between honour and evil lay an area best avoided, since it raised unease and suspicion in the strictly upright mind. This world was peopled by artists, by writers, musicians, philosophers; a world that defied understanding and was therefore held in contempt. Contempt was safer than wonderment, as it placed you secure on your pedestal and did not threaten the standards upon which tradition was raised. For tradition was proven worthy, it behoved its stalwart supporters to avoid exploring the avenues where its bitterest enemies lay.

Godliness was supremely important, defined by strict church attendance and acknowledgement of the scriptures without exploration or doubt. And the God who smiled on tradition was not at all affected by that other contentious issue, the existence of rich and poor. The rich, the rich by tradition, were clearly divinely selected, their power and acceptance of it was blessed by the presence on high. It did not cross the minds of the faithful that the lowly birth of the Saviour might be read as a condemnation of this attitude of mind. One's daughters did not marry carpenters, the very thought was ridiculous; that Our Lord was brought up by a carpenter had nothing to do with the case. You could still be an excellent Christian: at Christmas, look how lustily you sang of a babe in a manger, born in the humblest way to a girl who (though now elevated to the peerage as Our Lady) had admittedly been nothing more than a common village lass? You could overlook this graciously, seeing no implicit lesson, no anomaly in declaring yourself a Christian soul while knowing yourself superior, and ensuring your line did not integrate with village girls or carpenters, itinerant preachers or Jews.

All this Victor had subscribed, or rather acquiesced to; such attitudes and convictions were part of the rules of the club; to sit around brooding about them would be waste of time and disloyal to your family, to tradition, to your band of jolly good chums. But lately, quite often lately, he had found himself unsettled, ill at ease with the opinions he would once thoughtlessly have professed, and today his confusion had surfaced; he was suddenly miserably conscious that, entirely against his wishes, his life had changed its course and that the new one was perilous, leading into unknown waters, where the landfall was only a mirage and the calm bay full of sharks.

It was a distressing sensation. He felt exposed and forsaken, resenting the new strange loneliness, and recalling the conversation that had brought it to a head; a conversation he should not have heard, on which he had eavesdropped innocently, expecting nothing derogatory from the discourse of his friends. He had been recharging the glasses in the drawing room after the service, and had gone to fetch new bottles from the ice buckets in the hall: returning, he paused on the threshold, waiting for a tactful moment to invade the group round Lofty who were half-screened by the door. Standing there, savouring his party, he had listened absentmindedly, only gradually growing conscious of the meaning of their words.

"Seen William?" he heard Basher saying, and then he had leaned towards Lofty and added in a loud whisper, " 'Fraid Hester's not taking it well."

Lofty had laughed. "Who *is*, Basher? Be honest, the whole thing's a tragedy." He drained his champagne glass gloomily and added, "Bloody sad."

"Still can hardly believe it," said Alistair, shovelling down a handful of olives.

"Can't you?" replied Lofty sourly. "The whole place seems different to me. Can't feel comfortable in it. Something to do with the atmosphere. Queers and Jews and actresses all popping out of the cheese." He sighed, gazing over the parkland. "Jamie shouldn't have died, that's the trouble. I mean everyone knew that Jamie liked a little bit of skirt. But he didn't marry them, did he? Didn't bring them down here to embarrass us? And now there's an heir. Poor old Hester! That's done for her. Bloody sad."

"Can't believe it!" repeated Alistair. "I mean the child particularly. Bad blood. And now he'll be stuck with it when the marriage falls apart. William gave it two years at the wedding, and he wasn't far wrong by the looks of it. But of course that's neither here nor there now she's produced a son."

He had surged forward then with his bottles, his face set in a smile, his mind seething with amazement and indignation at what he had overheard. All through lunch the words had scalded him, and his anger, slow to kindle, had grown as he watched his friends sitting there eating and drinking his wine; had grown as he looked up the table and saw Miriam, bored and silent, and Ian beside her quite openly eyeing the contours of her breasts. 'Jamie didn't marry them, did he?' Did that make him worse than Jamie? Was it worse to fall in love with her and then to make her his wife, than to lust after her like Ian, with the subtlety of the farmyard, while your suitable spouse kept your household and allowed you to father your brood?

'Bad blood, and now he'll be stuck with it.' Oh Lord, before whom all are equal. They had all said Amen to that, hadn't they, as they knelt in the church today? Dismally, he remembered the first weekend when Miriam had come down at his invitation to join a houseparty at Coombe. They had all gone to church at Coombe Basset, and she had berated him afterwards, saying how could they all stand there singing such a savage and bloodthirsty psalm? She had nearly walked out . . . As he had not noticed the words himself he had nodded, but had been alarmed by her vehemence, 'Don't you go to church much?' he had asked. 'To church? To hear that mumbo-jumbo?' she had laughed and shaken her head. 'Just look round this lot, will you darling? Would they have the face to come here if they thought about what they said?' He had not taken that remark seriously, her absurdity was so charming and the 'darling' so unexpected that he let the matter rest. But perhaps she was right. How could Alistair, in view of his expressed feelings, have possibly stood Godfather to Miriam's son today? And the others too, with the sole exception of Dorothy . . . that was when he had glanced towards her and found her dealing with Dickie in her usual helpful way.

Now as he stood talking to William he noticed that she was missing; he had felt that a little chat with her might have kept his anger at bay. 'William gave it two years at the wedding.' Yes, it hurt, the treacherous bastard! He would show him he had not blundered when he made his marriage vows. He had chosen his wife and he'd keep her, for better or worse as he'd promised. Whatever the cost in friendship, he would make them eat their words.

He glared round. His guests had arranged themselves as they always did after coffee: the men in groups by the windows, the women nearer the fire, each sex relieved to have won through to that peaceful hour of enjoyment when it ceased to be socially necessary to talk to each other's spouse.

The men were swapping anecdotes. Patsy guffawed with laughter. Basher, his face empurpled by wine and the heat of the fire, urged an imaginary hunter towards the back of the sofa, while Ian and Lofty applauded. Yes, the party was going fine. Liz and Amy were deep into children; Jean Arbuthnot and Bunny talked labradors; Aunt Eleanor, diamond encrusted, held court from her high winged chair. As he watched this group, Hester detached herself, and crossing to the windows, began to pull the curtains, with a brisk proprietorial air.

His family, his companions, relaxing naturally round him, the atmosphere suddenly easier than it had been the whole day. Could he bear them ranged against him? Endure the sense of exclusion? Was it after all inconceivable to admit a mistake had been made? But of course it was too late anyway, for as Alistair said, there was Jamie . . . He swung round, furious, terrified at the self-knowledge he had plumbed. Where was Miriam? Where the hell was she? Her place was here beside him. He would find her and he would teach her what he expected of his wife.

He went into the hall. No Miriam; only Dorothy, near the telephone. Maybe they'd been together?

"Where is Miriam?" he said.

There was no reply and he realised that his voice had been high with anger. He really seemed to have startled her. Poor old Dollie! He tried again.

"Seen Miriam around lately?" This time he was consciously gentle, but good God, she looked peculiar! Perhaps too much champagne?

Distressed, he stepped towards her, but the sound that escaped her halted him: too small a sound to be called a scream, or even described as a cry; a sound shrill and faint as that of a wounded rabbit; a horrible noise, despairing, agonised. For a second he stood there motionless. Something awful had happened to Dollie. But the sound was – well, bloody scaring, though he couldn't quite say why. And then, as he strove to gather his wits, she suddenly bolted past him, and before he could move to stop her, had disappeared into the night.

16

Was it seconds ago, or minutes? Two or three. It could not have been more. Or could it? She had no conception of how long the power had held her at its mercy in the void. It could have been hours, a lifetime. Yet the images coalesced as if not an instant parted them: that of Victor, tall and stern as an avenging angel, with his awful accusatory cry, and the wraith-like figure of Miriam, now vivid, now insubstantial, the figure that in her madness she had seen as destined to die. But the moment when she had come to herself, aware and sane in the wilderness, how long was it separated from the moment the power held sway? She did not know: Miriam grating and swinging round bends in the avenue; Miriam cursing the traffic beneath the arch of the gates; Miriam hurtling onwards, hectic and fragile and foolish, the straight road familiar before her; Miriam at the bridge – all the visions were equally plausible, all equally impossible, only one fact was absolute, one certainty remained, that if she did not overtake her, that if she could not stop her, then Miriam would perish and she would have caused her death.

Dew had fallen, the steps were slippery, and she skidded, almost falling, but the windows shone out on the gravel, and she stumbled towards her car and flung herself into the driving seat. Her keys? They were in the ignition. Would it start? Her fingers trembled, the car often refused to start; but the engine fired obediently, harsh and strident in the silence, and with unaccustomed mastery her foot coaxed it into a roar. She shot forward, feeling the gravel explode and scatter beneath her, the pebbles squealing and grinding at the sudden bite of the wheels. She flicked on her lights; mist was rising from the lake and from the river, and the separate beams of her headlamps pierced a wall of wispy grey. She surged into it, peering intently down the two converging tunnels, and they opened to engulf her as the avenue rose and fell.

All physical fear had left her, for what could compete with the terror that Abbot's Bridge held in store for her if she had not followed in time? If she was too late to save her? If already she had killed Miriam? Killed her because she hated her for being Victor's wife. That terror possessed her utterly, and she drove without fear or caution, correcting the car automatically as it skidded and slewed and swayed. Her whole mind was bent on discerning the glint of Miriam's tail lights, which surely, despite the terror, must appear round the next bend?

Trees loomed up and vanished: the huge cedar on the corner, the chestnuts that meant you were past the stable yard, the avenue of lime trees that formed an unbroken tunnel, until the rhododendrons at the bottom of the hill told you the lake was approaching with its maples and its rushes; it was like a familiar poem, she knew it all by heart; every bend, every bump, every pothole, every place where the gradient altered, every bush where an overhanging branch might lash against the car.

But there were no lights. She had built her hopes on picking them out when she reached the lake, where the road curved round the margin and the trees gave way to grass. Instead the fog was impenetrable; she craned forward, hunched over the steering wheel, straining to keep the car off a verge which she now could barely see. Once or twice she felt her tyres spinning in the treacherous squelch of the mosses, and she jerked the wheel wildly to right herself and swerved back on to the track.

It seemed to go on for ever; she became aware of her body, the chill in her clamped muscles, the pain behind her eyes. Years had passed since hope had propelled her like this without care for her person, and she knew it was starting to fail her as she left the lake behind. Her hands were beginning to tremble, her skill and command to desert her, when the rising ground of the avenue caused the pall of the mist to thin and she saw the two red pinpricks of Miriam's lights ahead of her, tiny, faint; could she be mistaken? But no, they were growing fast, and suddenly blazed orange. Brake lights! The car must be waiting for the traffic to pass on the main road. As she swept on up the hill, she could see it beneath the arch of the gates in the glow of its own headlamps. Each second made it more certain that the prize was within her grasp.

She no longer felt tired; she felt braced, exhilarated. An old confidence came back to her, a confidence she had known years ago when she was young and strong, and the future before her had promised adventure and fulfilment round every bend of the road. Now this road, though dark and hazardous, was offering a challenge, and she had risen to meet it; this time she would not fail. She could drive fast, faster than Miriam; she was free of all constriction, the agonies and confusions had suddenly dropped away. Free! She was free from Victor. Free. She had seen and recognised the cataclysmic outcome of her obsessive love. She had recognised its folly, its hopelessness and its passion, a passion so insidious that it had obscured her sight, and finally all but destroyed her; until blinded by self delusion she had justified her own motives for the harbouring of such hate that she had descended to murder. But reprieve had come in time for her; she was free, her mind was clear again and she could reverse her fate. She was granted a new beginning, a renewed and glorious liberty, the world was bathed in its radiance: she would remake her life, sell the house, accept Aunt Maud's offer, take the job at Gaston Abbey; perhaps when she was settled she would even start to write the sequel she had intended to *Pathways to Comprehension?* The prospect widened indefinitely as she drew nearer the lights. She would resurrect old friendships, apologise to Humphrey; it all seemed so simple and natural now that she was free.

Abruptly the brake lights flickered, then went out. With shocking suddenness Miriam's car had vanished and the gates were left empty and dark. A stab of panic ran through her: she had thought the ordeal over, had planned to draw up beside her in the crescent of the arch. Now she must follow her farther, and delay would mean disaster. She surged up the rise without slowing and drove straight on to the road – one moment of naked terror, her body braced for an impact, and the confidence rushed back, vindicated. This time she would not fail.

Yet time had grown short. She knew that now it was only measured in minutes. She set her hazard lights flashing and jammed her hand on the horn. Surely Miriam must have noticed her? Yet Miriam's speed did not slacken, though the distance between them was shortening as the seconds ticked away. Was she deaf? Was she blind? But of course Miriam was neither: she saw her and she heard her, she simply would not give way. She enjoyed driving fast, and particularly she disliked being overtaken, all her conceit and obstinacy would be fatally, fully aroused. She was not going to stop for anything unless she was forced to do so, and to force her meant to frighten her; no other course remained. Even Miriam would set limits to a possible speed for negotiating the bridge at Abbot's Corner and the corkscrew bend beyond. Even Miriam would avoid a car she saw bearing down behind her, set on direct collision if she held to her pace on the road, a car that was moving so quickly that to match its speed would be suicide, a car driven by a madman, entirely out of control.

Dorothy hesitated: for the inside of a second the freedom dangled before her enticing and attainable, and then with numb resignation she released it, and watched it go. Watched it go, melting, vapourising and vanishing into nothingness. She crushed the accelerator till the metal rasped the floor.

Speed snatched at her like a whirlpool, she was sucked into its vortex. Sight and sound and all experience spun crazily round in its shell: the flame of Miriam's brake lights, sunshine blazing on brass in a chancel; Victor's voice in the echoing hallway, the screech of tyres on the road; the fear of no longer believing in a creed that demanded allegiance, the skill that she had to summon as she whirled past Miriam's car; a wild jumble of impressions – night opening before her, and then the concourse of faces that lined the tall hedgerows.

There was Father, nodding and smiling, with his mitre

hovering above him and his face as young as a curate's; Mother sitting up in bed, with Nurse Rose standing beside her and holding out an infant, wrapped up like a gypsy's baby in Miriam's evening shawl. Humphrey stood, reading from a lecturn; as she passed he looked earnestly round at her. He was trying to tell her something, but she could not hear what he said. A pity. What a pity . . . Miriam opened her wardrobe and Justin stepped out of it shrouded in a cloak as dark as the night. He was holding a bunch of flowers; as he vanished she recognised it as a bouquet that she had gathered one spring-time long ago in the meadows behind the manor, with Victor striding beside her. And now Victor, dressed for hunting, was standing in the road.

"Would you like me to come with you, Dollie?"

Kind Victor, who did not desire her, who did not in the least understand her; kind Victor who loved his wife. She smiled at him sadly and tenderly. She was near the heart of the whirl-pool, she could hear the sudden silence, feel a weightless airborn sensation as she plunged into its core. Freedom. "I'll go alone, Victor. I'll be quite all right without you."

She was glad to see he believed her. She did not fear the dark anymore.

17

Miriam sat in the morning room with her back to the empty terrace, and stared at the correspondence that choked and cluttered her desk. 'Mother's desk', as Hester still called it; a lovely piece of furniture, veneered on oak in tulip-wood and purple-wood and kingswood, with a background of mahogany for the delicate floral design. At first, seeing how it pained Hester, she had taken quite a pleasure in swamping its exquisite features in a slatternly array of old catalogues and programmes, fashion magazines and order forms; but deliberate baiting of Hester was no longer a game she played. It had lost its savour years ago, and the strained atmosphere between them was now just one more tiresome aspect of the struggle of living at Coombe.

She looked at the mess apathetically. There was so much that needed attention: invitations that must be answered, household bills to be sorted and paid, the guest list compiled for the party, winter clothes ordered for the children, a letter to Amy MacKenzie thanking her for last weekend. Their own shoot was coming up shortly; she should really make all the arrangements, choose the food and see the servants, before they set off again for the long drive to the Arbuthnots; Victor wanted to take up the horsebox, so they would have to leave in the morning to get there before dark. Anyway, the beds were comfortable. She yawned, picking up her pen. It was dreadful, this fog of lethargy; Victor hated idle indifference, though her pregnancy made some excuse for it – three babies within four years. And of course there had been the accident . . .

'Dear Amy, What fun we had with you! A super weekend. Who else can . . .' She lifted her hand. Be so bossy? So intolerant? Such a bore? She wrote on: '. . . give such marvellous parties?' She wished there was someone to laugh with, to exchange congenial comment, to see Amy through her eyes. (A sour one that, little lady. Wouldn't be her old man for a pension. Must be like living with a lemon that somebody's squeezed dry.) Odd, how much she found she missed Dickie. But Victor had set his limits, and had simply refused to countenance his bringing Cheryl down. She supposed he knew that she visited them when she went up to London, and that despite the embarrassment, she was glad he had married again. What if Cheryl *had* been a stripper and still dressed as if she was twenty, so long as she cherished Dickie and made him look happy and well? It was foolish to think him diminished by their very humdrum existence, the pub and the supermarket and the cheap decor of their flat; more foolish still to be jealous because an elderly chorusgirl now filled the prime position she had always held in his life. She could not have coped with Dickie; it was bad enough without him, for Victor had grown exacting and expected his house to run well. The accident seemed to have changed him, he had grown much harder to satisfy, had become less gentle and thoughtful, and grew angry if he was crossed. Angry and cold and impatient, as if he had never forgiven her, though she knew her attempts to save Dorothy spared her the full weight of his wrath. Her scramble down the embankment, her futile efforts at rescue, the fall she sustained in the process, the injuries to her head – in some measure all this compensated for her failure to find a reason for the wild irrational joy-ride that had led to Dorothy's death.

All the same, he held her responsible. And Dorothy was a heroine. It was obvious that Victor felt a great deal must be made of a life paid for so dearly. Well, at least she had made the babies. She knew he was proud of Jamie, though sometimes with Imogen . . . She threw the pen down violently. She must learn not to be so silly: there was no reason, none whatever, for Victor to think such a thing. Indeed when she found she was pregnant the very month after the accident, she herself had dismissed the outside chance that the baby might not be his. It had somehow seemed quite impossible, in the wake of such trauma and tragedy, to face up to any dilemma, to cause further crises and pain. She had not had the strength or the confidence to risk losing Victor and Jamie, or to come to a decision to contact Justin again. She had needed all Coombe's security to restore her self-possession, to blunt the realisation of what Dorothy had done.

'How sweet of you to have Imogen. Victor tells me I was naughty to bring her, when Nanny could easily have looked after her at Coombe. But since she was ill in the summer, I find it hard to leave her. You were so kind to put up with her. I hope you didn't mind.' She paused, staring down at the paper: what rubbish it was. She knew Amy had been outraged to find that Imogen had invaded her smart weekend. Children had not been invited, and since Amy's were all at boarding school there was now no nursery structure to keep toddlers out of the way. It had been a social blunder, and Victor had not understood it; but then the last thing she wanted was for Victor to understand the extent of her feeling for Imogen. It might even start him wondering why his fair-haired sensitive daughter was so little a Templeton, in temperament or appearance. Thank God he had taken a week up North with Ian for the grouse shooting, and had missed the moment her baby fat had suddenly melted away with the dehydration of fever, so that suddenly and heartrendingly she had found herself looking at Justin's high-boned, finely structured face. Heartrending. She had resented feeling anything so intensely, and the strength of the resemblance had given her a bad fright. But at least Victor had not seen it, and now when the child was near her she felt less inert and leaden than she had for a long time. Though the wakening was painful, it tantalised and compelled her as though Imogen was a window in the gloom of a prison wall. A window too small for escaping . . .

She got up and looked over the garden, fallen leaves clogged the flags of the terrace – how she loathed this time of year: the floods and the gales, and the poignancy of the clear brittle calms that followed, the thin air and the mists in the evenings, and the first suspicion of frost. She touched the scar at her hairline, as if she half expected to find again the disfiguring gash that had run from temple to chin. At times like this Dorothy's hatred flooded over her like a poison, a hatred beyond comprehension, that left her completely unmanned. Dorothy had wanted to kill her; kindly, gentle Dorothy had lied to her and hated her enough to desire her death. She had tried to erase the knowledge, to pretend it had been a nightmare, born of the shock of seeing a car scream past her and plunge off a road that had inexplicably vanished. Sometimes she believed her own story, that another reason existed for the fact that she had been there. A reason she had forgotten – the blow to her head, amnesia. Sometimes, but not in October. Three years ago today.

Pheasants called harshly from the coverts. Basher was coming to dinner. Three figures appeared in the garden, making an erratic way to the steps that led to the terrace. Nanny upright as a ramrod; Jamie square and solid, brandishing his inevitable toy gun; and Imogen, skipping lightly and carelessly in between them, amazingly sure of her movements for a child not much more than two. She hardly seems like a baby, Lizzie had said disapprovingly. But now, with the new baby coming, her attention had left Imogen. An odd little thing, best forgotten, though for Victor's sake one naturally hoped the child would turn out satisfactorily. When one thought of Cousin Grace . . .

A door slammed. Victor's step in the passage. He was back from his morning rounds early, and she braced herself for the moment when he would tap on the door, a meaningless piece of etiquette like most of his good manners: he had every intention of coming in, so why did he knock at all? Tap, tap. Her teeth clenched together; she had heard her own voice too often, the indifference or the testiness implicit in her 'come in'. She continued to stare through the window, though already she could smell him. Autumn woodsmoke from the plantation; from the stud, the reek of horse.

"I hope you're a little better?"

She turned round with resignation: he had asked her to come to the stables, and she had said she felt ill. How lucky he had reminded her, one forgot these polite excuses as easily as one made them.

"Oh, much better, thanks," she said. "I expect it's just that I'm broody."

He looked doubtful. "You should get a tonic. I mean, heaven help us, Miriam, you've not even opened your mail!"

"I could see nothing interesting in it." Thank you letters. Invitations. Bills and circulars. Begging letters from a charity or two. A note in Lizzie's writing that she knew would contain the suggestion that she should pay them a visit as soon as the baby arrived.

There had been nothing to stimulate her in those mounds of correspondence since that letter from Annabel asking her if she could get away for a quick trip to Vienna, for the festival: 'Everyone is going,' she had written, 'all the usual crowd. If you would come and join us it would be like the old days.' Victor had laughed when she told him. 'Good Lord, what a weird suggestion! Doesn't she know that you're married?' No more remained to be said. He did not tell her he forbade it, that would have been most uncivilised, and since Miriam had no money, unnecessary as well. He knew she must agree graciously, since any overt battle would reveal her complete dependence in a most unflattering way.

She knew now her last words would have riled him; he could not bear her indifference. The best that she could hope for was that he would go away. But to her dismay he seated himself on a gilt chair, newly upholstered in a delicate primrose satin, and stared at his wellington boots. They were muddy and straw adhered to them. His unconscious arrogance maddened her, the way he abused the furniture, the way he planted his feet squarely on the Persian carpet as if it was a doormat.

"I've been thinking," he said to the carpet. "I've been thinking, all this morning . . ."

How very unusual, Victor. She bit back the retort.

He went on. "I mean, Jamie's christening was three years ago exactly. All that business with poor old Dollie. Not a happy sort of day. Makes you think. Well, your mother dying, and the accident, and the babies ... I think you've borne up magnificently. You've had a pretty rough ride."

The children appeared to be fighting. Jamie lifted his gun to hit Imogen. She could see his face grow crimson as Nanny intervened.

Victor said, "You need a holiday. Would you like to go away with me, just the two of us together? When you've had the baby, I mean. A sort of second honeymoon. We could go anywhere you wanted to. I could take you to Vienna. Or we could go farther afield."

He looked up, his face flushed and eager with a childlike appeal that moved her, against all inclination, by its transparent hope. But to travel alone with Victor! He could, by his sheer Englishness, reduce any exotic setting to a travesty of Coombe. What on earth would they do? What experience would not be dulled by his presence? They had not gone abroad together since they were on their honeymoon, and as far as Victor was concerned it might as well have been Brighton: the fascination of Florence was contained in their bedroom. She remembered the trips with Justin, cheaply planned, but rich in fulfilment. Even those vulgar holidays with Dickie on the yacht that he'd bought as a status symbol had been exhilarating. What the hell, eh, little lady? After all, life was meant to be fun.

Fun. Imogen reached the terrace, placed one hand on the parapet, and holding the other before her, stood gravely upon one leg. She wobbled and nearly fell over, recovered herself determinedly: watching her from the window, Miriam held her breath. Will you leave this extraordinary pageant and come to America with me? The pain was so unexpected that it brought the tears to her eyes. And yet she was filled with tenderness; and a strange anticipation, as if after years of rehearsal she had turned up the clue to a wearisome part that had seemed to be completely beyond redemption.

She looked again at Victor. In the afterglow of the tenderness, she could almost pity him. It was hard for him too, their marriage, now that Dorothy's intervention had destroyed what opportunity they once might have had to part. Was that what she had intended? Had Dorothy known about Justin? Had she been in love with Victor? Surely not? But what does one know about other people's feelings? 'The country air's done for your acting . . .' Could she still put on a show? At least Victor was undiscerning, credulous, the perfect audience.

"Oh darling, that does sound wonderful!" Surprised. Delighted.

Not bad.

And gratitude too. She held out her hand and let the tears spill over. "I can't tell you how I would love that. You're always so good to me."